BOUNDLESS FRAGMENTS- A COLLECTION OF A NOVELLA AND SHORT STORIES

I0564456

BOUNDLESS FRAGMENTS- A COLLECTION OF A NOVELLA AND SHORT STORIES

J. A. Springs

The small things usually begin to add up over time.

Introduction:

We can all remember that Jack and Jill went up the hill to fetch a pail of water, but what do we really recall about the story beyond that simple rhyme? What do we truly know about Goldilocks besides her preference for everything being "just right"? These stories are memorable, yet it's not the plot that stays with us—it's the human emotions and reactions, or the lack thereof, that leave an imprint.

It's those emotions, those reactions that make a story resonate. Think back to a moment in your life, perhaps at a game where your team won with a last-minute score. What do you remember most clearly? Is it the smell of beer on the breath of the person sitting next to you? The clothes they wore? Or is it their raw, unfiltered reaction to that winning score, the joy and excitement that mirrored your own?

This, to me, is the essence of storytelling. You can have the most fantastical plots, well-developed worlds, and all the technical prowess in writing, but if the characters fall flat—if they don't *feel* real—then the story fails to achieve its purpose. It's the authenticity of human emotions and responses that make a story worth reading.

The Importance of Character Development

When I write, I focus on developing characters that feel real, not just to me but to my readers as well. Realistic characters are more than just names on a page—they're individuals with desires, fears, flaws, and hopes that readers can connect with. Whether a character is facing supernatural forces, struggling with grief, or experiencing the joys of parenthood or just parenting in summer heat, their responses need to be grounded in reality.

Realistic characters affect emotional connections because they give readers someone to root for, someone to relate to, or even someone to dislike. It's the complexity of human emotion that makes a character memorable. When readers see themselves reflected in a character's choices, struggles, or triumphs, the story becomes more than just entertainment—it becomes personal.

Realistic characters are real *because* of how they are—just like real people.

The Clock and the Curtain was born from a writing exercise I set for myself: to create tension, drama, and character depth without the use of dialogue. In this brief but heavy moment, everything rests on what isn't said—small gestures, held breaths, and choices left hanging in the air. By removing spoken words, I was able to focus entirely on body language, silence, and emotional undercurrents to show the weight both characters carry. The emotions remain real, even when unspoken.

The Neighbor grew from an attempt to capture emotional vulnerability without relying on grand gestures or exaggerated romance. Inspired by the depth and intimacy found in John Legend's *All of Me*, I reversed the familiar narrative dynamics, allowing the woman to be the one quietly, patiently reaching.

This is not a story of sweeping declarations, but one of quiet attention, subtle connection, and unexpected tenderness. At its heart, it's about seeing and being seen—without artifice, without pretense. We come to know the male narrator through his own reflections, but through his eyes, we also glimpse a woman whose presence and quiet persistence carry genuine emotional resonance.

Without Saying, Your Bag's by the Door was born from a writing exercise that challenged me to convey a character's emotional shift through a single, symbolic gesture. What began as a test of subtlety evolved into something more—a quiet, aching exploration of love, fear, and the silent understandings between people who truly know each other.

We often imagine that revelation requires language. That closure comes through explanation. But some truths arrive in silence, not because we're unwilling to speak them—but because we don't need to. In this piece, what is not said becomes more important than what is. A bag by the door becomes the message. A hug becomes the conversation. The absence of a fight becomes the answer.

Fractured Reflections grew from an intensely emotional nightmare—not because of horror or supernatural terror, but because of the profound anxieties it stirred. Originally imagined as a horror piece, I ultimately chose to discard those elements, realizing they risked distracting from the deeper truth I wanted to explore.

Instead, I kept the emotional intensity, grounding the narrative in the quiet, personal turmoil of self-doubt, shame, and healing. The unease is no longer external; it's internalized within the characters themselves. It's not the external circumstances that matter—it's how the characters carry the weight of their fears, their regrets, and ultimately, their hope.

It Is What It Is was a thought experiment in writing a scene that simply *is*. It doesn't pretend to be anything more than what's on the page. It has a simple plot. It makes sense. It captures something real.

Keep it simple. Make it entertaining. Avoid abstraction. That was the challenge.

This scene proves that writing a moment well—no drama, no metaphor, no hero's journey—isn't harder than writing an entire plot. The moment feels true to life. Anyone who's suffered through a brutal, humid summer without AC—especially as a parent—will instantly relate. That groggy, heat-induced lethargy; the way everything becomes a competition just to stay sane; the resigned humor of it all... it's familiar, grounded, and honest.

Two men. It's hot. They complain. One dumps water on the other. Then they return to the same stillness they started in. That's the whole arc—and it's enough. Sometimes, nothing happens. And that's the point. It's about how it feels to exist in a moment like that.

Holding On is a narrative born from my own exploration of grief. Losing someone close during my teenage years made me question how individuals process loss and how it affects those around them. The characters in this story are driven by their need to cope with and understand their grief, and it's their very human responses that make the story impactful.

Grief is a universal experience, but it manifests differently in everyone. By focusing on the nuanced ways my characters handle their grief, I aim to create a narrative that feels both unique and relatable.

By Innocence Commanded began as a simple writing exercise, one intended to explore character tension in limited space. But as the exercise unfolded, it revealed a deeper narrative—one I felt compelled to expand. This story is not about youthful naivety, nor is it a meditation on lost innocence or moral struggle. Rather, it is about conviction. It asks what happens when a king—young in years but not in resolve—fully assumes the weight of sovereignty without hesitation or doubt.

The world may view him as innocent because of his age, but innocence does not define him; it merely surrounds him. Internally, he is something far more: a sovereign who knows exactly what must be done—and does it.

In *A Gift From Heaven*, for example, the story is deeply personal to me. After being blessed with three sons, I always hoped for a daughter. This story reflects that journey of longing finally coming true.

The emotions in this tale—joy, wonder, fulfillment—are drawn from my own experiences, and I hope they resonate with readers who have felt similar desires.

How Realistic Characters Build Emotional Connections

Creating characters that feel real allows readers to form emotional connections with them. When a character's emotions are authentic, readers are more likely to empathize with them, to feel their pain, joy, fear, or triumph as if it were their own. This emotional connection is what keeps readers invested in the story. It's what makes them care about what happens next, what makes them turn the page, and what makes them remember the story long after they've finished reading.

In all the stories in this collection, my goal has been to create characters who feel real, whose emotions are genuine, and whose experiences resonate with readers. Whether it's the longing for a child, the pain of loss, the fear of failure, the weight of unspoken duty and sacrifice, the absurdity of unbearable heat, or the quiet vulnerability of unexpected connection, these stories explore the depths of human emotion. This emotional connection is what keeps readers invested in the story. It's what makes them care, turn the page, and remember long after they've finished reading.

Encouraging Reader Reflection

As you journey through this collection, I encourage you to reflect on the characters and their experiences. Consider how their emotions and responses mirror your own, or how they differ. Think about how the themes of longing, grief, fear, and fulfillment play out in each story, and how these emotions connect the characters, regardless of the genre.

Ultimately, my hope is that these stories will evoke a range of emotions in you, the reader. That you'll find yourself moved by the characters' journeys, that you'll see parts of yourself in them, and that you'll carry their stories with you long after you've turned the last page.

The Clock and the Curtain

The sunlight beamed through the gauzy curtains, muted and suffused—soft and revealing at the same time.

Connor sat on his side of the room, arms loosely crossed. His brows pinched together, but the furrow softened beneath a faint, hollow smile. His breath came deep and slow, his shoulders rising and falling with an uneven rhythm.

Marcy sat across from him. The space between them was barely a few feet, but it felt endless. A low table separated them, simple and ordinary, yet suddenly immense.

The sunlight spilled across her more fully, catching the tear tracks glistening down her cheeks. She clutched a handkerchief in her lap, fingers twisting the delicate cloth without pause. Her gaze never lifted to meet his.

Behind them, faint sounds filtered in from beyond the heavy oak door.

The distant click of heels grew louder as they crossed the marble floor outside. Then a knock—soft, respectful.

A maid stepped cautiously into the room, carrying a tray with two glasses of water. She hesitated as she saw them—neither of them speaking, neither acknowledging her presence.

Her voice broke the fragile quiet. "Forgive the intrusion, Your Highnesses. The lady requested something to drink earlier. I thought you might need it now."

Connor offered the smallest nod as she set the tray gently on a side table.

The maid lingered a moment longer, her eyes shifting between them. She cleared her throat. "Preparations continue, my lady. The seamstress will arrive shortly with the last adjustments for your gown."

The soft ticking of the mantel clock punctuated her words.

Still, Marcy didn't move. She kept her head lowered, fingers twisting tighter. The thin fabric strained beneath her grasp.

The maid paused again, as if sensing the weight in the room. Then she tried to offer something lighter. "The procession from Kaldrith will arrive before sundown, as expected. His Grace travels well, I'm told. His retinue is most eager to meet you, my lady."

The breeze from the open window slipped inside, catching at the loose strands of Marcy's golden hair, brushing them gently across her cheek. Connor's gaze followed the movement, and for a moment, his hand twitched—an impulse to reach forward, to tuck the errant lock behind her ear. But he stayed still.

The clock ticked louder. Slower. The silence felt deliberate.

The maid drew in a careful breath. "Your father asked me to remind you, my lady—once His Grace's arrival is announced, the formal presentation shall begin. The families will expect your blessing before the final papers are signed."

Connor's jaw tightened. His shoulders rolled ever so slightly, a faint tremor passing through him before he stilled again. His arms unfolded, hands resting on his knees now, as if ready to rise but not yet daring to move.

The maid lowered her eyes, sensing her presence was no longer needed. She dipped into a shallow curtsy and backed away. "If you require anything further, my lady... Prince." Her voice softened. "I will leave you."

The door whispered shut behind her.

They remained.

The ticking returned to fill the space she left behind, steady but somehow heavier.

Marcy's breathing hitched once—a faint shudder that passed through her shoulders. Her head turned, slowly, just slightly toward him.

Connor leaned forward, the movement barely perceptible. His eyes followed the faint quiver at the corner of her mouth. She seemed on the edge of speech—but nothing came. Only a silent exhale. Her gaze faltered, lowering again.

A few long seconds passed. Then, with a suddenness that seemed to defy the stillness, Marcy stood. She turned quickly, leaving the handkerchief behind on the table as she hurried from the room.

Connor remained seated, his hands loosely folded in his lap.

The clock resumed its measured ticking.

Afterword: The Story in the Silence

This piece was born from a writing exercise:

Create an emotionally powerful scene that reflects the beliefs and positions of two characters—with no dialogue, internal or external.

It wasn't about building a world.

It wasn't about establishing plot.

It wasn't about dramatic stakes or clever structure.

It was about **resonance**—and whether characters could become real to a reader *without* ever speaking.

And somehow, they did.

We don't know what Connor and Marcy went through before this moment. We aren't told what decisions lie ahead. They aren't debating anything aloud. But we **feel** it.

The weight between them.

The silence stretching.

The restrained movements, the failed glances, the subtle ways they nearly reach for each other and don't.

That silence *is* the story.

This scene earned its place as the first work in the anthology because it quietly demonstrates the entire purpose of this collection: to create characters who feel real—whose presence lingers even after the page ends.

This story doesn't rely on revelations or resolutions. Its power rests in what's withheld.

And that is where its truth lives.

Why This Piece Opens the Collection

This story isn't here because it explains anything. It doesn't. You won't learn the full history of Marcy and Connor. You won't even know the full weight of what they've lost or what they're about to sacrifice.

But you'll *feel* it.

That's why it belongs here—**because it achieved what the exercise demanded and more.** Because without a single spoken word, without the reader knowing their backstory, these two became *real*. The page blurred. They stepped off of it.

You see it in the twitch of Connor's hand. In the tightening of Marcy's fingers. In the breath that almost becomes a word but doesn't.

And in the silence that says far more than speech ever could.

This is how the entire anthology works—not through elaborate plot or high concept, but through **resonance**. Every story in this collection is designed to reach past the skin of narrative and into the reader's emotional core. Each one asks a different version of the same question:

Do you feel this?

Why It Was Chosen

This story matched that mission so clearly that it couldn't be placed anywhere but first. It prepares the reader—not thematically, but **emotionally**—for what follows.

This is not a tale about events. It's a tale about impact.

And not on the world—but on *you*, the reader.

The work functions like a quiet test: *Will you connect with them even when you don't know them?*

If the answer is yes, then you're ready for what's to come.

The Neighbor

The weather was brisk. It was getting towards the end of winter and I had somewhere to be. Medical appointment. About an hour's drive to the nearest Veterans Affairs hospital. Not where I normally went but I needed to see a specialist so... that's where I went.

I stepped outside to a strong gust. Pulled my hat down closer on my head so it wouldn't fly off. One of the problems of living in a small cities—row homes clustered so close together, facing one another across a two lane major road. Damn wind tunnel effect.

I looked up in the sky. It wasn't looking real good.

Damp. Grey.

Plus the chill.

I shivered as I pulled my door closed and locked it. I glanced up once again. Ozone filled my nostrils, overpowering the exhaust trapped close to the street.

It was gonna rain within a few hours. I looked down the street where I was parked and back up again. I heard a whistle and realized I'd let out a breath I'd not known I was holding.

I'd have to fight to find a parking spot when I returned. Likely have to park around the corner and get soaked walking the block back to my house. Couldn't be helped. I'd lived here a few years and... That was just the way of it.

Looking at my bike parked up on the curb, next to the house, I debated taking that for a few seconds before coming back to reality. That would be foolish in this weather.

Not for the cold alone.

The cold and the rain.

Not a good mix.

I stepped off the porch. That's when it hit me. The noise. Not from the street and cars passing. A conversation across the street. I looked.

People I'd not seen before. Moving truck was parked half crooked against the curb.

New neighbors I'd reckoned. Just one more set of bodies to occupy the space in between. That was the first time I saw her.

Hoodie.

Leggings.

I blinked.

Damn long legs and dark hair and, from what I could hear but not make out, a bright voice.

I peered just enough to get a bearing on the people and went about my way.

She stayed with me.

In my mind. In my thoughts.

Wasn't because I thought she was pretty. I had to admit she was gorgeous though, but that hadn't kept her in my thoughts.

I shook my head. Went back to my rambling thoughts of what kept her in my mind.

It was those eyes.

Those eyes that smiled at me when she noticed me glance her way.

They were warm and they smiled even though a smile never touched her lips.

A month later, it was starting to get warmer. It wasn't anywhere near summer yet, just a warm front passing through.

I'd gotten up early. Much too early. Being retired, I had no need to work. So I didn't.

It wasn't a job I left the house for. I'd run out of creamer so I was going to the convenience store at the end of the block.

This city up north was old. It was something I couldn't explain. I'd never grown up in a city like this. Convenience store on both ends of the block. I'd seen movies about New York and the inner city so it was easier to think of them as bodegas.

Anyway, I'd just locked the door.

Nobody called my name. Hell, no one on the block even knew my name.

But. I had to turn.

Something.

No. Someone... I felt someone call for my attention.

I turned. She was there. Just across the street.

Blue jeans. Light jacket. Hands stuffed in the pockets. Her hair flowing over her shoulders.

She smiled.

She waved, hesitantly.

I waved back. Sort of an automatic thing. Felt like something I should just do. So I did.

That wasn't what was weird.

When I stepped off the stoop of my house, I caught her in the corner of my eye. She was looking both ways up and down the street. Then she sort of sprint-jog-speed walked across the street.

"You going to the store?"

I blinked.

"Uh. Yeah. To get creamer."

"Let's go."

I stared a moment. She didn't say anything more. She just turned and walked to the closer of the two stores. I followed.

I felt my brows tightening. I watched as she seemed to skip happily in front of me. It didn't just seem weird. It was weird.

It was definitely awkward, but I tried not to make too much out of it. I was just more or less curious why this... What? Twenty? Maybe twenty-five? Year old girl had just suddenly decided—out of the blue, to escort me to the store. I just shook my head and followed.

I only had one thing to get. It was too damn early in the morning for heavy thinking. I'd rather have my coffee and cream than have to have deep thoughts that early so I let it go.

We got to the shop quickly. She watched me pick out my creamer, pay for it, and walked with me back towards my house.

In the end, there was no explanation. No other conversation even. She waved and crossed the street and went in her house.

I went in mine.

A few months later.

Yet again, I had somewhere to be.

Strange though. I don't leave the house that often at all. Grocery shopping—every two months. Medical appointments—once or twice a month.

Not a big deal. I didn't think I had health problems. I was a few years over fifty. Retired, twenty year, disabled vet. So yeah, I figured I had to keep on top of my health with screenings.

VA recommended an all. Not my choice.

I also only had one other place I had to be at least once a month. I had to go see my parole officer.

I wasn't proud of it. I'd screwed up a few years earlier. That's why I was stuck in this city.

I'd just crossed the street—started walking towards my car, when I noticed steps behind me. Someone slipping into an easy pace beside me.

I saw a deep pair of brown eyes first. Felt like I'd dropped down into them. A smile followed that.

It was her.

"Hey, I need to go up the street. Can you give me a ride."

I just glanced up the street. Not meaning to. It dawned on me that this girl threw me off my stride.

I did what people do— acted automatically, without thinking. Mentioning up the street meant my eyes had to look that way. I thought about the wave that time she followed me to the store.

I frowned. I hated doing that automatic thing.

I turned to face her.

"It's not far. Just up the block to the pizza place up there," she continued.

Yeah. I knew the place.

It really was just two blocks away. The direction she wanted to go was downhill from where we were but then, that immediately turned upwards for the rest of those two blocks.

I'd made that walk. Before I'd gotten my car.

I didn't like it. Especially in the summer.

I gave a half smile.

"Sure," I said.

It wouldn't cost me anything to give her a lift. I wasn't gonna be late. The downtown area is where we lived. Well, at least just at the periphery. The parole office was literally a five minute drive. Giving her a lift wouldn't put me out of my way.

"Get in," I said as we got to the car.

I reached out and opened the door. She slipped in. Turning to regard me as she lifted her legs. I didn't know if that was a question in her eyes. I closed the door behind her.

'Pretty thing', I admitted to myself.

That was it. I didn't think anything else. I dropped her off and went about my business.

Early summer seemed to come with a fury.

In the south, it's usually a subdued affair. Something just a little less jarring. Not up north.

When those northerlies passed through with a warm front, boy where they warm. It wasn't even June and the temperature jumped from the high fifties to the low eighties.

Weather man said it would pass though. I believed him. I'd lived up here long enough to witness it. It just reminded me that I couldn't wait to leave.

I had to admit I'd rather deal with the clinging humidity of the south. It clung to you like a blanket in the summer but I felt that was better than dealing with the weather swings this far up north.

Soon as I'd opened the front door it seemed like I walked out into a circus. She was standing outside her door, screaming at some young guy.

Spanish. I'd already made the guess that she had some type of hispanic heritage. Didn't know from where though. And I wasn't close enough to her to feel like I could ask. I guess the real reason was, I didn't want to get close enough to ask.

After five years of living in that house, I couldn't even tell you who any of my neighbors were. I knew there faces. I assumed they knew mine but none of us knew one another.

Anyway. The argument seemed heated.

I registered the guy. I'd seen him a couple of times.

She'd be standing in the doorway talking to him sometimes. She'd be getting out of his car—coming from somewhere obviously, sometimes.

It didn't concern me. I just registered it.

PTSD made me do that.

Hyper vigilance.

I had a love hate relationship with it. Cursed the fact that I still had to deal with it, considering. The last time I'd seen combat was almost fifteen years earlier.

I started to turn my gaze away from the domestic scene. I didn't want to intrude. I laughed silently because I couldn't even figure out how the hell I would have intruded anyway. It was in public.

Her eyes caught me.

I froze.

She'd gone quiet. Right in the middle of whatever the hell she'd been saying. She stood there, arms crossed, the door to her house open behind her.

There wasn't a smile in her eyes this time. I felt stupid even considering one might have been.

It wasn't my business. My feet started to move.

I turned in her direction a final time. Her eyes fell to the ground and for a second... she seemed to hesitate. Then it seemed like she made up her mind.

I watched. Transfixed again.

She said something to him. Her voice seemed empty. Like she'd given up the fire she'd had earlier.

I at least understood enough Spanish to know she told him to go fuck himself.

She walked into the house and closed the door while he stood there still ranting.

I walked off, went to my car, heading to where I needed to go.

Two weeks later, the heat was on the upswing and it wasn't because of a warm front. The weather turned. This was farming country. It always got like this.

Rainy.

Downpour.

Then drizzle.

Almost for three months straight.

You'd think the bottom of the sky had been split open and someone forgot to turn the water off. But, that's just how it was.

It was late into the evening. I was sitting behind my desk writing.

That's what I did instead of working. Not to supplement my income or anything. It was to fill the emptiness in the house.

The sound of the clicking of the keyboard was consistent.

Monotonous.

It filled the space. Well, at least it did until I heard a knock at the door.

I stopped and looked up. I doubted what I'd heard was real or not. I didn't know anyone in this state, let alone this city.

I looked over my monitor, but both my cats were laying on the carpeted floor in front of my desk. It hadn't been them thumping up and down the stairs.

I listened again.

The rain pattered in the alley between my house and the next. I could hear it from the window behind me.

The knock returned.

You'd expect that when a knock wasn't responded to, it'd get louder. It didn't. It was softer.

I slowly pushed back from the desk and went down the stairs. I unlocked the door and stepped back, not knowing what to expect.

I wasn't expecting her.

She stood there.

The rain fell slowly.

Softly.

Consistently.

The same damn drizzle that always found its way through the leak in my laundry room roof.

Her arms were tight in front of her. Hands clutching her elbows. Her gaze fixed on the step leading into the house. The white t-shirt she wore was damp and it revealed more than I wanted to see.

I looked down her body. I couldn't help it.

I'm a man.

I also wouldn't have called those shorts that she had on beneath that cropped t-shirt. Too damn short for that. If anything, I would have guessed that this was an outfit she would have worn to bed.

My voice came slowly.

Rough. Coarse.

Even to my ears.

"You wanna come in."

She didn't say anything. She just nodded.

I released the door handle and stepped back. I couldn't step aside, the hallway was too narrow for that.

She came in.

Slowly.

Reaching behind herself, she grasped the door with her hand and instead of facing it, she just slowly backed up until the door was closed. Her back resting on it.

She'd still not looked up into my eyes.

I didn't know what to do.

There was a loud thumping in my ears. My chest seemed to be tighter than it should have been.

I waited.

The sound of the fridge hummed. A beep from somewhere in the house registered in my head. The silence clung like her wet shirt.

I watched her shoulders lift.

A small voice followed.

"I waited." Her voice barely registering.

I leaned forward.

"What?" I said slowly.

"I was hoping that it worked," she said softly. A bit louder than before.

I'd leaned forward to make out what she was saying but now I felt myself listing backwards.

"What worked?"

She didn't answer. I turned my head to my feet, distracted, as I felt something brush up against my leg. One of my two feline companions.

My eyes were drawn to her again. To where her voice echoed softly in the hallway again.

"I liked the look in your eyes."

I felt my throat work. It felt like I'd been sucking on a cotton towel with how dry my mouth was. I couldn't figure out why I swallowed, but I had.

This one sided conversation was confusing the hell out of me. I didn't have a clue what she was trying to say and didn't even know how to ask her to be clearer. So I said nothing.

"You saw him that day, didn't you?" she asked softly.

I nodded. I had an idea of who she was referring to.

"You're not like... them," she finally said.

Silence drifted in again and I wondered if she still had more to say.

She did. I listened.

"You don't look at me like other guys do. You seem to see me, instead of look at me."

That topped it. I was lost.

My fingers were digging through my hair before I realized it.

"Look," I said, taking a further step back. "I have no idea what... this," I gestured and kept speaking, "is, but you're gonna have to speak a bit clearer. I mean, um. Make more sense."

The sound of a car passed outside. Then another. This late at night, the traffic was slow, so those two cars were well spaced apart. I didn't know how much time passed between hearing both of them, but it wasn't a little.

I watched her arms fall to her sides. Her gaze came up to meet mine.

"I just wanted to know if it worked?"

I was getting frustrated.

"Know if what worked?"

"Me making you fall in love with me."

My mouth worked open and closed.

A breath.

No.

Two.

She'd covered the distance between us shortly after that.

She fell into my arms.

What came next. I wasn't expecting it.

She kissed me.

Gently.

It's been a year now. I opened the door and came into the house.

I turned back into the hallway after locking the door behind me.

"Welcome home," came a soft voice.

I looked up.

Saw her eyes.

I smiled.

It's been a year now. I opened the door and came into the house.

I turned back into the hallway after locking the door behind me.

"Welcome home," came a soft voice.

I looked up.

Saw her eyes.

I smiled.

Afterword: The Girl Across the Street

I didn't write this to be a love story.

In fact, I didn't know what it was when I started. Just a man. A neighbor. A moment. Some odd tension in the air. I followed that.

There's no plot here, not in the traditional sense. No twists. No grand events. Just a series of almost-silent interactions, glimpses, gestures, and internal observations. The kind of moments that don't usually make it into fiction because they don't seem like they matter.

But they do.

Because this story isn't about **what happens**. It's about **what builds**.

It's about presence.

And how presence—when held consistently enough—starts to mean something. Even if you never quite know what.

This man doesn't chase anything. He's not seeking love. He's not performing. He doesn't believe he has anything to offer, and he's not sure if he wants anything from anyone. He's just living—**quietly, resigned, distant**.

Until she shows up.

Not with declarations. Not with demands. Just... with attention.

And over time, that attention accumulates. A smile. A wave. A walk. A ride. A knock on the door.

How I Pulled It Off

I didn't write this like a traditional narrative.

I wrote it like **memory**.

I built the scenes around normalcy—*errands, weather, casual thoughts, unspoken trauma*—because that's how real connection often shows up: **while you're living your life, not while you're looking for it**.

The story doesn't ask for your excitement.

It asks for your **patience**.

It wants you to sit with this man through the mundane long enough that when she arrives, she doesn't feel like a plot device—she feels like a question. Like maybe she doesn't belong. Like maybe she *does*.

And then I let the relationship unfold in reverse.

No exposition.

No romantic gestures.

No dramatic tension.

Just presence. Just weight. Just quiet.

The man doesn't know how to name what's happening. And neither does the reader. That's by design.

Because connection often doesn't come with labels or clarity at first. It comes with *confusion*. With hesitation. With wondering whether a wave means something. Whether a smile matters. Whether someone showing up at your door means they've come to stay—or just needed to be seen.

I didn't want to explain her. I didn't want to explain him either.

I just wanted you to feel what happens when someone **keeps showing up**, and another person **finally lets them in**.

Why It Matters

If you felt uncertain through this story—unsure of what she wanted, unsure of what he felt—good.

If you weren't sure whether this was romance, or loneliness, or healing, or habit—better.

Because that's what it was meant to be: **an atmosphere** of fragile, unexplained resonance between two people who don't quite know what they are to each other, but who both recognize that it means something.

This isn't about what they become.

It's about how they arrived in the same place—quietly, without knowing exactly when.

Sometimes love doesn't announce itself.

Sometimes it just knocks, quietly, in the rain.

Without Saying, Your Bag's by the Door

"We could go to your parents' place after the semester ends," Melonie said, stepping around a woman wrangling two toddlers near the bakery window. "Your Mom's already planning some kind of cookout—she says you still owe her a rematch in dominoes."

I laughed low under my breath. "She cheats."

"She's just competitive."

"She hides bones under napkins."

Melonie grinned at me sideways. "She's fifty-six and needs wins where she can get them. And I like her.

There was a twinkle in her eyes as the smile reached them. "More than I like you, I think."

I shrugged and put on a straight face. "It's her charm."

She punched me in the arm and kept walking.

We passed a flower stall. I reached out without thinking and nudged a tulip back into its vase. The whole day had that kind of rhythm—easy. Natural. Like the steps we were taking belonged to something solid between us.

"So how long are we talking?" I asked, brushing my knuckles against her hand. "Just the weekend? Or..."

"Longer if you're off," she said, not missing a beat. "I mean, we haven't had more than a day or two to actually beanywhere since spring break. And that didn't really count. You were gone half of it."

I nodded. "Yeah. Okay. Yeah, that sounds good."

And I meant it. I was already picturing it—her mom calling from the kitchen, the uneven porch out back, the way Melonie curled up on that ratty couch like it was her favorite place in the world.

We veered into this little storefront. One of those spots with scented candles, glass trays, notebooks with clever gold lettering. Melonie stopped at a shelf and tilted her head at this ceramic lamp shaped like a cat mid-stretch.

"This is either hideous or perfect," she said.

I squinted. "That's both."

She laughed. "Maybe for the study nook?"

I opened my mouth to mess with her about our growing zoo of animal-shaped décor—then my phone buzzed.

One short vibration.

I glanced down: Pickup time confirmed. 0700. Return TBD.

It was the same day we were supposed to go to my parents' place.

I didn't move. Not right away.

She was still turning that lamp in her hands, checking the price tag. She didn't say anything. Didn't even glance my way.

I tapped the phone off and slid it into my jacket pocket. By the time I looked back up, she was saying, "I think this would go great with that desk lamp you found."

I hesitated a beat. "Yeah," I said. "Yeah, that'd work."

Then she looked at me.

Not mad.

Not hurt.

Just... looked.

Like she saw everything. Like she already knew.

I met her eyes for a second, maybe less. There wasn't anything to say.

She smoothed her fingers over the lamp base one more time and set it back on the shelf.

Then she smiled—soft, easy. "We should check out that place across the street. The one with the chocolate-covered pretzels."

I nodded. "Yeah. Okay."

And just like that, we moved on.

But something stuck.

Not what she said.

Not even how she looked at me.

Just the space between it all.

We didn't go home after we left the shop.

We grabbed those pretzels. Walked a bit more. Talked about everything and nothing. She never brought up the message. I didn't either.

But it hung there—between us. Not in an angry way. Just... still. Unnamed.

Eventually, I said I was gonna meet Mike. She nodded, kissed my cheek, told me not to stay out too late.

She also reminded me that she had a class to get to.

I watched her walk off, bag of pretzels swinging at her side like nothing.

Now I was sitting in a bar, nursing a warm beer. Mike sat across from me—good company, but not much for conversation unless it was his third drink or later. We weren't there yet. But we were close.

I hadn't gone home because I didn't know how to walk in the door and tell Melonie something I hadn't fully figured out how to say.

So I called Mike. Told him I needed a beer and didn't feel like drinking alone. Truth was, I needed help putting words to the thing I already knew was going to hurt her.

Mike caught my sigh and glanced over.

"Damn, Doug," he said. "You know I don't do these heavy conversations. And I'm guessing that's exactly where this is headed."

I gave him a half smile. Gotta hand it to the guy—he wasn't wrong.

He never was, when I called like this.

"I got exams tomorrow," he added, shaking his head. "And here you are, getting me drunk the night before."

My hands were wrapped around the warm beer in front of me. I watched the foam clinging to the inside of the glass, drifting slow and aimless at the edges.

We'd reached that point—the one where I could finally unload the thing sitting heavy in my chest. Mike was already talking more. That was always the cue.

"Spill it," he said after a sip.

Even before I was ready.

I looked up and caught the familiar look of resignation on his face. Resignation that masked a quiet kind of loyalty. The little smirk he gave wasn't sarcasm—it was reassurance.

He was a good friend. And I needed that right now.

"I got another gig," I said, voice low.

He knew what I meant. We'd all been tight since our first year in college. He'd heard enough to fill in the blanks.

The driving job.

It paid stupidly well—too well to pass up, especially for a full-time student without time for part-time anything else. But it always came with next to no warning. I'd get the word, and then I had maybe a day, two if I was lucky, before I had to be gone.

Most runs only took a day or two. Sometimes longer, depending on the route. It was all legal. Technically. Nothing shady.

Just messy. Unorganized. Last-minute.

It made keeping up with classes hell. But I turned in everything on time. Crushed my exams. Nobody had a reason to question it.

Except Melonie.

And now this new job was scheduled the same day we were supposed to head to her parents' place.

The only real problem was Melonie.

She didn't like the damn job. Hated it, actually. But she knew why I took it—knew it paid for school and our apartment. She understood that much.

Didn't mean she had to like it.

Melonie and I loved each other. Been that way since junior year of high school. We even chose the same college just to stay together. We shared everything now—classes, bills, space.

But...

"The next driving job starts tomorrow. I have to tell Melonie tonight," I said.

Mike shook his head and set his glass down. "Damn."

I shifted under the table, the crunch of peanut shells under my shoes louder than it should've been.

"Why don't you just get another job?" he asked. "Something easier."

We both knew the answer. It wasn't like we hadn't had this exact conversation before.

"You know I can't," I said. "Where else am I gonna find a gig that pays enough to cover rent and tuition? I make more doing this than I ever would folding shirts at some store. And I don't even have to clock in for half the week."

He didn't answer. Didn't need to. I wasn't really asking.

And I knew I wasn't funny—but I said it anyway:

"Pays more than a 'part-timie jobie' for less than a 'turd' of the work."

Mike didn't laugh. He never did.

But he kept talking.

"This sucks, bro. I don't know what to tell you," Mike said, cracking open a peanut and tossing it into his mouth.

He wasn't wrong.

We both knew the real issue. It wasn't about cheating—Melonie trusted me. It was about me being gone. The leaving. The silence in between.

At first, she handled it. Said she understood. And she did, I think. But the more I had to go, the harder it got.

Melonie had her own history with loss. Her parents—both gone before she was thirteen. Then her aunt, not long after we finished high school. That was it. Everyone who raised her, gone. One by one.

So now? Now she holds tight to what she has left. She clings to it. And when I leave for days at a time, even if it's for work, I can feel it tearing at her.

She never says it like that. Not anymore. In the beginning, we talked it through. But over time, those talks turned into arguments. Then the arguments turned into silence.

Now, when I say I've got a job, she just nods. Cold. Quiet. I leave. I come back. We carry on like nothing happened. But that silence between us—that's what's killing me.

And the worst part? I don't have an answer. I don't have a solution. I can't give up the job—we need the money. I won't let her work some part-time gig just to keep us afloat. Her degree comes first. It has to.

So yeah, it sucks. All of it.

Her degree took a hell of a lot more out of her than mine did. Labs, lectures, group work—attendance wasn't optional. Meanwhile, I could skate by on submissions and exam scores.

Still, I couldn't shake the guilt. Like I was failing her somehow. Not because I left, but because I hadn't helped her feel safe in the leaving. I hadn't eased the part of her that worried I might not come back.

And the truth was—I didn't know how.

That night, sitting across from Mike with a beer that had gone flat in my hands, nothing felt different. I still didn't have answers. Just the same dull ache sitting behind my ribs, dragging me down.

We didn't talk much after that. Not because he didn't care. There just wasn't anything left to say. Nothing either of us could offer that would make things better—for me or for Melonie.

Mike had even tried helping, early on. Checking in on her while I was gone. Stopping by to keep her company when my jobs ran long. But even that eventually stopped working. Some things couldn't be fixed from the outside.

Another hour passed. Three more beers between us.

Finally, we stood, muttered our goodnights. Mike waved down a shared ride. I just headed upstairs.

The bar was on the ground floor. Our apartment sat right above it.

And tonight, I wasn't in any rush to open that door.

I stood at the apartment door for longer than I probably should've. My head wasn't spinning from the beers—it was the thoughts, the weight of what I needed to say and how to say it. It was still early evening. Melonie should've been home from class by now. Probably starting dinner.

I took a breath, unlocked the door, and stepped inside.

She turned as I came in, catching me mid-thought. She looked beautiful—barefoot, wearing one of my t-shirts that hit mid-thigh like a dress, her hair pulled up, casual and effortless.

The thing drowned her. Like a damn nightgown. Small-ass girl, always made my clothes look oversized and stolen. I smiled.

I knew from experience she probably had nothing else on but underwear beneath it, and it made me smile. Not in a lustful way—just that quiet, familiar warmth. The way you smile when someone makes a space feel like home.

"I already started dinner," she called out from the kitchen doorway. "Got your text about meeting Mike downstairs. Figured you'd be home by eight."

Her voice was light. Easy. Like everything was fine.

I closed the door behind me and shrugged off my coat, tossing it over the arm of the couch. Then I crossed to the kitchen to help. She didn't need much—just a few plates to bring to the table.

That part was easy.

The rest wasn't.

We sat. Melonie moved the cat out of the way—he'd climbed into her chair like he owned the place, waiting for attention. I smiled again, but it faded just as fast. My chest tightened with the thought that I'd have to ruin this quiet evening with what I had to say.

I was a lousy dinner guest.

Mostly, I listened. She talked about her day—classes, professors, some girl in her study group who couldn't stop flirting with the TA. I picked at my plate. My answers came right when they needed to, just enough to keep the rhythm going, but I wasn't present. Not really.

My shoulders ached with the weight of it.

Eventually, we finished eating. Shoulder to shoulder at the sink, we washed dishes like always. I kept my eyes down, focused on the swirl of suds around my hands. I could feel it in her now too—that shift. The awareness. She knew there was something. Something she probably wouldn't like.

I tried to speak. Just a breath, the beginning of a word.

She kissed me instead.

Soft. Brief. Final.

Then she turned and left the kitchen without a word, leaving me behind with the last few dishes to rinse. When I dried my hands and stepped into the living room, I saw it:

My small travel bag. Sitting by the front door.

Melonie was standing there. Quiet. Her hands were clasped behind her back, eyes fixed on her own shifting feet.

"Why's my bag there?" I asked, cautious. I wasn't sure what was happening. Maybe she was asking me to leave. All I knew was it felt like someone had punched me in the chest.

She didn't answer. Just stepped toward me—slow, steady—until she stood a foot away. Then she stopped.

Nothing happened for what felt like forever.

In that silence, I heard everything. The ticking of the clock. The distant rush of traffic through the window. Maybe even the dull thud of my own heartbeat.

Then Melonie moved.

She wrapped her arms around me. Rose onto her toes and kissed me—soft, brief, full of something I couldn't name. Then she whispered, "Come back home safely, okay?"

She smiled. Not wide. Just enough to hold me together. Her hand slipped into mine.

"Let's go take a shower and get ready for bed," she said, gently tugging me after her as she turned toward the hallway.

Fractured Reflections

Chapter 1

Dr. Evelyn Harper walked toward her office. The rhythmic clack of high heels resonated against the polished granite tiles, the only cadence in her life she had a sense of control over. Her thoughts drifted back to her morning lecture. The freshmen had been eager, wide-eyed, still convinced they'd change the world—one patient at a time.

Her shoulders lifted, and a breath escaped. She ran her hand through her hair and recalled her own youthful idealism—the belief that she could make a difference. It seemed that with age came disillusionment. The stark reality of the world had eroded her optimistic veneer. No rose-tinted lens could obscure humanity's capacity to transition from saint to sinner, from kind to cruel. And in a world like that, staying hopeful—especially as a psychologist—was getting harder every day.

Each day blurred into the next—different classes, yet the same hollow outcomes. She yearned to retreat into the solace of research, where she could contribute without confronting the complexities of human nature face-to-face. Writing research papers provided a sanctuary where statistics replaced sorrow, and citations didn't cry at night. A realm where she could fulfill her professional duties, free from the emotional toll of patient interactions.

Evelyn had barely sunk into her chair when her phone vibrated, cutting into the fragile quiet. She preferred it that way—no jarring ringtone, just a subtle buzz. Discreet. Controlled.

The caller ID flashed a name she hadn't seen in years: Steve. An old friend from college. She kicked off her heels and sank into the leather chair, her chest tightening.

"Hey, Steve," she said, her tone cautious.

"Evelyn, it's been too long," came the reply—slightly crackled but unmistakably him.

She leaned back. Already bracing.

"What's on your mind?"

It had been years. Of course he wanted something.

"Nothing much. I was just calling to catch up," Steve answered comfortably.

She pulled the phone away, brow furrowing. She checked the screen. The name blinked back at her. Persistent, of course.

Still Steve.

Still bullshit.

It wasn't going to change.

And his sudden desire to "catch up" seemed out of character.

This wasn't a friendly call. This was an ask.

She knew Steve. Consumed by his career. Family often taking a poor second best in his hierarchy of priorities. Friends? Ranked even lower. He seemed to keep them around only until they served some purpose to him. This call signaled such an occasion.

"Cut to the chase, Steve. What's the deal?" Evelyn's voice was calm, but her patience wore thin.

"It's not like that," Steve spluttered, feigning innocence. She didn't buy it. He was putting on a show—tailored for her benefit.

"What do you need?" Evelyn insisted, voice low and deliberate.

"Alright, alright," Steve relented.

She heard him release a breath. His frustration was audible.

"It's about a damn case I'm working on," he started, tone measured. "My client, Alex Mitchell, needs some help."

There it was. The ask.

The name tugged at Evelyn's memory, a faint recognition dancing at the edges of her consciousness. But the memory refused to cooperate. She ignored it.

"What's the deal with this patient? Why come to me?"

"I'm at my wit's end," Steve hissed through clenched teeth. She could almost picture him shaking his head.

"Alex is in a bad way, and nothing seems to be getting through to him. I need your expertise."

A heavy silence settled. Evelyn hummed, noncommittal.

Before she could speak, Steve cut in.

"I explained to Alex that I needed to bring in someone with more experience in his specific trauma. He agreed, which is why I'm reaching out to you."

Evelyn shook her head slowly. "Steve, you know I stopped practicing. I've left all that behind. Teaching and research are my focus now."

"I understand, Evelyn," he said quickly, urgency bleeding through now. "But this is different. Alex needs someone like you."

Steve knew exactly why Evelyn had left clinical practice. He knew what she'd walked away from—and why.

"Alex needs someone with your expertise."

Evelyn suddenly realized her hand was clutching her chest, fingers bunched tight in the fabric of her blouse.

She hesitated, caught between her disinclination to return to that life and the unbearable weight of inaction. The echoes of her former profession stirred—quiet but persistent.

"I don't even know who this Alex is."

"Alex Mitchell," Steve clarified, sensing her resistance. He lingered on the name, as if trying to nudge open a locked door.

"The artist. You've probably seen his work—magazines, gallery circuits."

Recognition flickered.

"The painter who's been making waves lately?"

"Exactly," Steve confirmed. "But there's more to him than the headlines let on."

Evelyn exhaled, long and heavy.

"Alright," she said at last, her voice steadier than she felt. "Where do I need to be?"

Steve perked up, the static line struggling to carry his excitement.

"Raven's Hollow. Just north of Harrisburg. Tiny place tucked near the Allegheny Forest. It's his hometown—like mine."

Evelyn grunted in acknowledgment.

"Send me his file. I'll head to Raven's Hollow. But don't expect miracles."

"Thank you, Evelyn," Steve breathed, the relief unmistakable. "I'll take care of everything. See you soon."

As Evelyn ended the call, she set the phone down and rubbed her shoulders. A quick glance toward the window—closed. Still, the air felt colder. Or maybe it was just the thought of returning to the work she'd left behind.

She turned away from the glass.

Evelyn stayed seated long after the call, her mind already racing ahead.

There were matters to attend to. First, the school. That would be simple—it was the end of the semester.

But Jerry... Jerry was another story.

Just days ago, he'd become her fiancé.

The memory of his proposal still sat awkwardly in her mind, like wearing a wool coat in summer.

The engagement wasn't the problem. She'd accepted it readily, as a continuation of their relationship.

She was devoted to him. She did love him.

It was what she wanted—wasn't it?

Evelyn gnawed at her lip.

The decision to leave—even briefly—would strain things. She knew it.

And the truth?

She'd been distracted—preoccupied with her own thoughts—long before he'd asked the question.

Sighing, she picked up the phone again.

Reluctantly, she dialed.

After a few rings, Jerry answered in his usual cheery tone.

"Hey, Evie, what's up?" Jerry's voice was warmth and excitement.

"Um, Jerry, I need to talk to you about something," Evelyn said.

A brief silence followed before Jerry responded. "Is everything okay? You sound...different."

Evelyn took a deep breath.

"I..." she began before hesitating. "Well, something's come up. I won't be able to make it to your parents' house in the Hamptons next week."

There was a pause on the other end of the line, and Evelyn could almost feel Jerry's disappointment through the phone.

"What do you mean, you can't make it? We've had this planned for months."

"I know, Jerry, and I'm sorry," Evelyn said, her voice tinged with guilt. "But this is really important. An old friend needs my help with a case. I..." she hesitated. "I can't just turn him down."

Jerry let out a sigh. "Evelyn, we've talked about this trip for weeks. It feels like you're always putting your work before us. I thought we were going to spend more time together, especially after the semester ends."

"I know, and I'm sorry," Evelyn repeated. She grimaced, feeling her heart sink with each word. "But I promise, we'll reschedule our trip. I just need to do this right now."

There was a long pause before Jerry responded, his voice softer now, tinged with resignation. "Okay, Evie. I understand. Just...let me know when you'll be back, okay? We'll figure things out then, I guess."

Evelyn felt a pang of guilt as she heard the defeat in Jerry's voice. "I will, Jerry. I promise. I'll be home soon to pack a bag. I'll see you then?" Her last question came out more like a question than a statement.

Jerry didn't respond immediately. She quickly added, "I love you."

"I love you too," Jerry replied, though his voice lacked its usual warmth.

As Evelyn ended the call with Jerry, her hand clutched her belly. She knew she'd just disappointed him, but beneath it all, there was a sense of relief. Relief that she wouldn't have to put on a façade of personal happiness during a week spent with Jerry's family. Time pretending her life was perfect when it wasn't.

She knew she was distancing herself from her own reality. But the allure of escaping to Raven's Hollow, even if it meant diving back into the world of patient treatment she had tried so hard to leave behind, was too tempting to resist. If helping Steve with the case meant she could avoid facing the harsh truths about her own dissatisfaction and disillusionment with her life; facing Jerry's expectations and the uncomfortable lies of happy smiles to his parents, then she was willing to endure it.

Jerry's parents, they were good people. She just felt so goddamn awful at having to put on a front for them.

Stepping back into the fray and seeing to a patient would come at the cost of her own comfort, but it was nothing compared to living like everything was alright. Perhaps, she hoped, in helping Alex Mitchell, she could find a semblance of meaning amidst the chaos of her own doubts and disillusionment. But deep down, she resented the idea of being pulled back into the world of therapy and patient treatment.

She pushed a pile of papers from the middle of her desk and slumped forward, head resting on the cool wood. The thought of facing the emotional weight of others' problems, especially when she struggled with her own, left her feeling weary.

With a heavy sigh, Evelyn pushed aside her conflicting emotions and focused on the task at hand. Raven's Hollow awaited, and she couldn't afford to dwell on things she didn't know how to fix just yet.

She gathered her belongings and prepared to leave her office. Jerry waited. Raven's Hollow waited. And maybe, just maybe, she would find a way to reconcile the fragments of her fractured life along the way.

Jerry wasn't at home when she got there. Evelyn thought that was for the best. She assumed he had just gotten an earlier start to go and visit his parents, seeking to avoid dealing with conflict when she got home. She packed her bags with the things she thought she'd need for the trip and headed out.

The landscape of central Pennsylvania unfolded before her like pages of a forgotten history book. Pennsylvania Route 666 wound its way through the rugged terrain, flanked by dense forests and rolling hills. The late afternoon sun cast long shadows across the road, painting the landscape in hues of amber and gold.

She was struck by the quaint charm of the small towns nestled along her route. Each town seemed frozen in time, with their main streets lined with historic buildings and cozy cafes and eateries here and there. The locals went about their business with a sense of familiarity, their lives intertwined with the rhythms of small-town living. As she passed through these communities, she wondered whether she was truly prepared for what might lay ahead.

There was the beauty of the Allegheny River, which ran parallel to her route, to distract her. Its waters shimmered in the fading light, a testament to the natural splendor of the region. Yet, beneath the picturesque appearance, she knew that this part of Pennsylvania bore the scars of its industrial past.

The remnants of coal mines dotted the landscape, their abandoned shafts serving as silent reminders of a bygone era. She felt a sense of melancholy as she passed these relics of the past, pondering the lives of those who had toiled in the darkness of the mines.

Evelyn found herself lost in thought, wondering what could she possibly hope to accomplish for Alex Mitchell, a patient she barely knew? And why had Steve reached out to her in particular, after all these years?

They had been little more than acquaintances in college, their interactions limited to the occasional nod of recognition in the hallways. They had attended a few parties together, exchanged polite small talk in class. They had even spent some few times, maybe twice, in professional partnership after graduation, but beyond that, their paths had rarely crossed. So why had Steve turned to her now, of all people?

The questions swirled in Evelyn's mind, elusive as the mist that hung low over the distant hills. But as she continued her journey into the heart of Pennsylvania, she knew that answers, like the truth, had a way of revealing themselves in due time. For now, all she could do was press on.

Upon arriving at Steve's house, Evelyn was greeted with a warm but distracted welcome. Steve's demeanor seemed preoccupied, his attention divided between her and the unseen worries that weighed on his mind.

"Glad you could make it. Was the drive okay?" Steve asked.

Evelyn smiled. "It was pleasant enough," she remarked. "The towns I passed are like something out of a storybook."

"Yeah, they have a certain charm," Steve replied absentmindedly. His gaze flickered to the door that he closed behind them before turning back to her.

As they made their way into the living room, Evelyn inquired about Steve's family, hoping to ease the tension with casual conversation.

"How's the family? How's everyone doing?"

Steve gave her a blank look.

Then shook himself and spoke.

"They're good. Thanks for asking. Actually, they're visiting my in-laws for a few weeks. Taking advantage of the school break to spend some time together. I figured this would be a good time to focus on work, especially with Alex's case."

His choice to stay behind spoke volumes about his dedication to his profession—and his disregard for anything else.

"Follow me. We're going to the guest room."

Steve led Evelyn through the house quietly.

"Am I staying here with you for the duration?" she asked, her curiosity piqued. She had expected him to arrange accommodations for her at a nearby hotel, but the lack of such options in the small towns along the way suddenly made sense.

Steve gave her a confused look. "Well, yeah. Is that gonna be a problem?" His brows furrowed slightly, sensing her hesitation.

"I just assumed..." She bit back her comment about his apparent oversight and instead simply nodded in acceptance, masking her surprise with a grateful smile. The prospect of having a roof over her head and the opportunity to rest before delving into the task at hand outweighed any discomfort she might feel about sharing accommodations.

"I'll give you some time to settle in. We can talk about things tomorrow," said Steve as he stood at the door before leaving.

The guest room was modest but tidy—'*overly tidy,*' she thought, '*as if no one actually lived in it.*'

Evelyn hesitated near the window of the room. The thought of diving back into patient care stirred a whirlwind of conflicting emotions within her. Tomorrow would undoubtedly bring new challenges and uncertainties, but for now, she could only mentally prepare herself.

The early evening had faded into night. The moonlight settled over the rooftops, and Evelyn watched the quiet rhythm of small-town life through the window. A dog barked in the distance, and a porch light flickered on across the street. It was peaceful here. Undisturbed.

Evelyn's gaze drifted to the house next door, its silhouette etched against the dimly lit night sky. Though not particularly close, she could still discern the faint glow of lights emanating from its windows. Someone moved behind the curtains, briefly silhouetted before disappearing. Just neighbors, living their lives. It was comforting in its normalcy.

Evelyn tried to get comfortable as she prepared for bed. She turned her attention to getting undressed and into her bed clothes. She scanned the room, and everything seemed normal—the quaint decor, the neatly made bed, the soft glow of the bedside lamp.

She sat on the edge of the bed and waited there a moment before pulling out her phone. Her fingers hovered above the illuminated screen after opening up the messaging app.

Sorry again about today. I love you. I'll call tomorrow. Promise.

She stared at the typed text. She wondered how Jerry would receive the words and then, pushed the thought aside. He'd receive it how he received it. Nothing she could do about that if she was going to send a text instead of call.

She set the phone down, turned off the lamp, and closed her eyes a moment, taking in the sounds outside the house. Crickets, that barking dog again. The hum of the refrigerator somewhere in the house coming to life.

For the first time in days, she wasn't pretending to be fine. She just didn't know what she was anymore.

She picked up the phone again and hit send before she climbed into bed and was quickly asleep.

Chapter 2

Evelyn awoke to the soft glow of dawn filtering through the curtains of her room. As she blinked away the remnants of sleep, a sense of fleeting refreshment washed over her before quickly dissipating. The events of the previous day felt like a distant dream, yet her purpose in this unfamiliar town lingered in the back of her mind.

"Am I ready for this again?" she mumbled.

Stretching languidly, Evelyn's thoughts drifted to the reason for her presence in Raven's Hollow. Steve's urgent call for help had pulled her from the safety of her routine, thrusting her into the midst of Alex Mitchell's enigmatic world. She felt apprehensive. A gnawing at her belly. She wondered if she was truly equipped to help another patient at this point.

Lost in contemplation, Evelyn's mind wandered to the incident with the next-door neighbors from the previous night. There was also something strange about it. The memory was hazy, obscured by the fog of sleep, but a sense of unease prickled at the edges of her consciousness. She pushed the thought aside, dismissing it as a figment of her imagination in the darkness of the night. Attributing it to fatigue from the long drive.

As she sat up in bed, Evelyn's gaze fell upon her suitcase nestled in the corner of the room. It served as a silent reminder of the life she had temporarily left behind—the comfortable routine, the familiar faces, and the obligations she had grown weary of fulfilling.

With a heavy sigh, Evelyn's thoughts turned to Jerry, her fiancé, and the strained relationship that lingered between them. It wasn't that Jerry was at fault; he was kind, supportive, and understanding. But Evelyn couldn't shake the sense of disconnection that had settled between them, like a shadow looming over their once vibrant relationship. She realized that it was likely due to her own actions in the relationship, having nothing to do with Jerry.

The upcoming trip to Jerry's parents' house in the Hamptons had loomed on the horizon, a prospect that filled Evelyn with a sense of dread. The thought of putting on a façade of happiness for a week, pretending that everything in her life was perfect when it wasn't, left a bitter taste in her mouth.

But there was another reason—a deeper, more personal truth—that Evelyn had chosen to heed Steve's call for help. It wasn't just about assisting Alex Mitchell; it was about escaping the suffocating weight of her own perceived failures. The memory of a former client, whose struggles she had been unable to alleviate, haunted her like a ghost from the past.

With a resigned sigh, Evelyn pushed aside her conflicted emotions and forced herself to focus on the task at hand. She couldn't afford to dwell on her own shortcomings, not when there were others in need of her expertise.

As she rose from the bed and prepared for the day ahead, Evelyn resolved to face whatever challenges awaited her. Perhaps in helping Alex Mitchell, she could find a way to reconcile the fragments of her fractured life and rediscover the sense of purpose that had eluded her for so long.

With a sense of quiet resolve, Evelyn stepped out into the morning light, ready to confront the day in this quiet town nestled amidst the Allegheny Forest. And though uncertainty lingered on the horizon, she hoped that perhaps, against all odds, everything would be okay in the end.

The morning sun cast a warm glow over the landscape as Dr. Evelyn Harper stepped out onto the porch of Steve's quaint home. She was greeted by the aroma of freshly brewed coffee, which wafted through the air, beckoning her inside.

"Good morning, Evelyn," Steve greeted her with a smile, holding out a steaming mug of coffee. "I hope you slept well."

Evelyn accepted the coffee with a grateful nod, taking a sip of the rich, dark brew. "Thank you, Steve. I did, actually," she replied, the warmth of the coffee soothing her frazzled nerves.

They sat in companionable silence for a while, Evelyn taking this time to wake up and get her thoughts together for what was to come through the day. Eventually, Steve, having the need to refresh his cup, stood and walked back into the house. Evelyn followed.

As they sat at the kitchen table, Steve gave Evelyn a brief overview of their plans for the day. "So, here's the deal," he began, his tone serious yet tinged with urgency. "Alex has a studio in the downtown area of Raven's Hollow where he works on his artwork. It's not far from here, just a short drive."

Evelyn listened intently as Steve explained the situation with Alex, her brow furrowing with concern. "He's been seeing me for complaints about recurring nightmares that trouble him immensely," Steve continued, his expression grave. "It's gotten to the point where he can't focus on his work or create new art pieces. I thought to reach out to you for this one since this is your area of expertise."

Evelyn felt a familiar sensation of commitment as she found herself settling back into the mind of an active counselor. A feeling she hadn't felt in a long while. It was oddly comfortable despite her reasons for leaving the profession at one point. Her brows furrowed. A sense of determination settled over Evelyn as she listened to Steve's words. She knew that helping Alex would not be easy, but she was committed to doing whatever it took to alleviate his suffering.

"Alright, let's head over to Alex's studio so I can meet him," Evelyn said, her voice firm with resolve.

With a nod of agreement, Steve rose from the table, ready to accompany Evelyn on their mission to help Alex. As they made their way out the door and into the bright morning sunlight, Evelyn couldn't help but feel a sense of anticipation building within her. Today marked the beginning of a new chapter—one filled with challenges.

As they climbed into Steve's car and set off towards downtown, Evelyn sat and stared out the window at the passing scenery. They shortly arrived at their destination.

The door to Alex's studio creaked open as Evelyn and Steve stepped inside, greeted by the faint scent of turpentine mingled with the earthy aroma of oil paint. The studio was bathed in soft, diffuse light, casting long shadows across the rows of canvases that lined the walls. The sunlight bathed the space through the large floor to ceiling windows lining the front of the establishment.

As they entered, Steve glanced at his watch, noting the time. There was no one around to greet them. "Looks like Alex is in his office," he remarked, gesturing towards a partially closed door at the far end of the studio. He stepped closer and peered inside, only to catch the sight of Alex busy fielding a phone call. Alex held up a finger towards Steve and gave a small smile.

Steve returned to Evelyn's side, his expression apologetic. "Looks like we'll have to wait a bit. Alex is on a call right now."

Evelyn nodded in understanding, her curiosity piqued by the vibrant paintings that adorned the walls. Without waiting for Steve, she made her way further into the studio, drawn towards the mesmerizing colors and intricate details of Alex's artwork.

Each painting seemed to pulse with life, the hues more vivid and electrifying than any Evelyn had ever seen before. It was as if the very essence of the subjects had been captured on canvas, their presence tangible and palpable.

"I can see why he's so acclaimed," Evelyn murmured to herself, her gaze fixed on the art that adorned the walls. Her fingers lightly brushed her chin as she absorbed the visual feast before her. Navigating around the freestanding partitions erected to create additional display space, she moved with quiet curiosity. Her footsteps resonated softly in the stillness of the room, each echo punctuating her growing fascination with the artwork.

But as Evelyn studied the paintings more closely, a sense of unease began to gnaw at her. The people depicted in the artwork wore expressions that seemed out of place—distorted, twisted into grotesque contortions that sent a shiver down Evelyn's spine.

Their eyes bore into hers with an intensity that made her feel as though they were peering into her soul, their silent screams echoing in the stillness of the studio.

Steve approached, smiling, breaking Evelyn from her reverie. "Impressive, aren't they?" he commented, glancing at the paintings with a hint of pride in his voice.

Evelyn hesitated, torn between voicing her concerns and waiting for Alex to finish his call. But before she could speak, the door to the office swung open, and Alex emerged, his troubled demeanor evident in the furrow of his brow and the tension in his shoulders.

"Sorry about that," Alex said, his voice strained. "I had to take care of some business. It's good to see you again, Steve. What can I help you with?"

Evelyn opened her mouth to speak, but no words emerged. She glanced at Steve, her uncertainty evident in her expression. Her curiosity about Alex's paintings was palpable—why did the subjects appear so distraught, as if tormented or even cursed? She wondered if Steve would dismiss her concerns or take them seriously. She felt it was crucial to address this to understand Alex's ongoing nightmares. It seemed that while Alex had channeled his troubling dreams into his art, there was something deeper at play. Evelyn knew that grasping this aspect was essential to effectively helping Alex overcome his recurring nightmares.

Before she could find the courage to voice her thoughts, Steve jumped in, steering the conversation towards Alex's artwork and the inspiration behind it. But as they spoke, Evelyn couldn't shake the feeling that there was something deeply unsettling lurking beneath the surface of Alex's creations—a darkness that threatened to consume everything.

Steve led Evelyn into Alex's office. She glanced around the dimly lit room, taking in the sparse furnishings and the faint smell of old books mingling with the musty scent of dried paint.

"Thank you, Steve," Evelyn said, turning to face him. "I'd like a few minutes alone with Alex, if you don't mind."

Steve nodded in understanding, his expression serious. "Of course. I'll wait outside. Just let me know if you need anything."

As Steve exited the room, Evelyn turned her attention to Alex, who sat behind his cluttered desk, his eyes weary and troubled. She studied him for a moment, taking in the lines etched into his face, the tension in his shoulders, and the haunted look in his eyes.

"Hello, Alex," Evelyn began, her voice gentle yet firm. "Thank you for taking the time to meet with me today. I understand that you've been experiencing some troubling nightmares and difficulties with your work because of that."

Alex nodded, his gaze fixed on the floor. "Yeah, it's been rough," he admitted, his voice barely above a whisper. "I don't know what's wrong with me. I just... can't seem to focus. I'm sure Steve told you about my nightmares? They make it difficult to concentrate during the day."

Evelyn listened intently as Alex spoke, her mind already turning towards the task at hand. The questions she needed answers to, relevant to her further assisting him to overcome this problem. She knew that before she could offer any assistance, she needed to understand the root cause of Alex's troubles—to unravel the tangled web.

"Can you tell me a bit about your childhood, Alex?" Evelyn asked, her tone gentle yet probing. "Were there any experiences or events? Any current difficulties?"

Evelyn listened intently as Alex spoke, piecing together the fragments of his story. His childhood sounded mostly uneventful. A few instances of bullying. Some struggles with self-worth. But nothing that immediately pointed to trauma. More likely: exhaustion. Stress. Overwork.

Yet beneath his words, there was something else. Subtle hesitations. The faintest moments where his gaze drifted off, as though something unspoken hovered behind his thoughts. Suppressed emotions perhaps, or unresolved conflicts he wasn't yet ready to voice. Evelyn mad a quiet mental note—not uncommon in cases like this. Often it wasn't just the stress itself, but what the mind was *avoiding* that field the unrest.

She leaned forward. "Alex, I dodo believe I can help. I'll only be here a short time—two weeks—but we can at least get started. Begin building something Steve can continue after I leave."

Alex's eyes widened with a mixture of hope and apprehension as he listened to Evelyn's words. "You do?" he asked, his voice tinged with a hint of disbelief.

Evelyn nodded, her gaze unwavering. "Yes," she affirmed. "But before we proceed, I need to speak with Steve further so we can come up with a plan that should help alleviate your symptoms, at the very least. From there, we can delve into the more compelling problems."

A sense of relief washed over Alex, hope flickering in his eyes. "Thank you," he said, his voice thick with emotion. "I can't tell you how much this means to me. It's been so long…" he trailed off as his voice hitched. His emotions overcoming him as the hope for relief became more hopeful.

Evelyn offered him a reassuring smile. "You're welcome," she said, rising from her chair. "We'll be in touch soon to discuss the next steps."

She glanced back at Alex, his smile appeared lonesome and troubled.

"Take care, Alex," she said, offering him one final nod before exiting the room. She made her way down the hallway, her mind shifting to thoughts of what she'd discuss with Steve.

As they stepped out of Alex's studio into the bright afternoon sun, Evelyn couldn't help but notice the curious stares of the residents of the city as they walked by. Their eyes seemed to linger on her, making her feel like she was misplaced. Not unwelcome, just unknown. A stranger to notice out of the crowd.

Steve, however, seemed oblivious to the odd behavior of the townsfolk, his attention focused on leading Evelyn to the nearby eatery he frequented often. "There's a great diner just down the street," he suggested, his tone casual as if nothing out of the ordinary was happening.

Evelyn followed Steve, her steps hesitant as she tried to shake off the sense of unease of unwanted attention. As they walked, Evelyn stole glances at Steve, debating whether to ask if the town regularly received visitors. But, before she could gather the courage to speak, they arrived at the diner, and Evelyn decided to put off the discussion for the time being.

Inside the cozy establishment, the scent of sizzling bacon and freshly brewed coffee greeted them, warming Evelyn's senses. She slid into a booth opposite Steve.

"Steve, there must not be a lot of visitors to this town. The people outside were staring at me," Evelyn said.

Steve glanced up from his menu, a puzzled expression crossing his features. "Hmm? Oh, I didn't really notice," he admitted, his attention already drifting back to the selection of dishes before him. "It's nothing to worry about. I guess they're curious to see a new comer in town. Plus, you stand out. You're rather attractive and dressed like you're going to work in a Fortune 500 company.

Evelyn looked down at her attire. Steve was right. She laughed lightly. "I guess I should have dressed more casually. I didn't think about that, though. I guess there'd be no reason to dress up like this in small towns like this unless you're going to church or something."

Steve nodded absently.

She continued to watch Steve peruse the menu and decided not to press the issue. They were both hungry, and Evelyn didn't want to ruin their meal with her observations.

So she pushed aside her concerns, focusing instead on the menu before her, determined to enjoy their lunch together.

After returning to Steve's home from their meal, Evelyn and Steve settled at the dining room table. She asked for a bit of clarification on the case Steve had called her for. Steve spread out his notes, a mix of scribbled observations and insights gleaned from his sessions with Alex, across the polished surface.

With a furrowed brow, Evelyn leaned forward. "He's clearly dealing with something and not getting enough rest. I'm not sure if your standard treatment methods will be enough."

Steve nodded, his expression thoughtful. "I agree, Evelyn," he replied, his tone measured. "I thought I'd find success with these methods. They're based on proven techniques that helped other patients overcome similar challenges based on other therapists studies."

Evelyn chewed her lip, mulling over Steve's words. While she respected his expertise, she felt that Alex's case required a more tailored approach. "I don't doubt the methods," she said carefully, "but this seems more complex than I initially thought. I think we need to consider a more personalized treatment plan."

Steve sighed, running a hand through his hair in frustration. "You're probably right," he conceded, his gaze meeting hers. "I just couldn't figure out what to do, you know?"

Evelyn nodded, sympathy softening her features. "I know," she said gently. "We'll approach this with a bit more flexibility and creativity."

Together, they delved into a brainstorming session, bouncing ideas off each other and piecing together a treatment plan that combined Steve's research, past treatment notes, and Evelyn's specialized knowledge. They discussed therapeutic techniques, potential interventions, and strategies for supporting Alex through his recovery journey.

As they worked, Evelyn felt a sense of camaraderie with Steve—a shared dedication to helping their patient overcome his struggles. It was something she'd experienced a bit in academia, but not like she'd felt when collaborating with others while in active practice. She knew their time together would be limited, but she was determined to make the most of it.

Finally, after hours of discussion and planning, they had a comprehensive treatment plan in place—one that they both believed would give the best chance at healing. With a sense of satisfaction, Evelyn leaned back in her chair, a tired smile tugging at her lips.

"Thank you, Steve," she said sincerely, her gratitude evident in her tone. "I think we're on the right track."

Steve returned her smile, a glimmer of optimism in his eyes. "I couldn't have done it without you," he replied, his voice filled with appreciation. "I'm confident that together, we can make a real difference now."

Evelyn couldn't was determined. She may only have had two weeks to work with Alex, but she was going to make every moment count—to offer him the support and guidance he needed to reclaim his life and find peace once more.

Chapter 3

In the quiet of the evening, as the shadows lengthened and the world outside settled into a hushed calm, Evelyn retreated to the guest room and dialed Jerry's number. With each ring, her heart pounded in her chest, uncertainty swirling within her.

When Jerry finally answered, his voice warm and familiar, Evelyn's resolve faltered. "Hey, Jerry," she began, her words hesitant yet sincere. "I'm sorry I couldn't go with you today. I know we had plans."

There was a pause on the other end of the line, and Evelyn could almost feel Jerry's disappointment through the phone. "It's okay, Evie," Jerry replied, his tone tinged with resignation. "I understand. We can always make plans for another time."

Evelyn sighed, guilt heavy on her. She wanted to tell Jerry the truth, to confide in him about the doubts and uncertainties that plagued her. But the words caught in her throat, and she hesitated, unsure of how to broach the subject.

Instead, she forced a smile, her voice tinged with forced cheerfulness. "Thanks, Jerry. I appreciate you understanding," she said, her words a feeble attempt to mask her inner turmoil.

Jerry's response was immediate, his love for Evelyn evident in his tone. "Of course, Evie. You know I have your back, no matter what," he said, his words a silent promise of unwavering devotion.

Evelyn's heart clenched at his words. She *wanted* to tell Jerry everything—to confess her fears and insecurities, to lay bare the truth of her disillusionment with her career and her life. But, she couldn't bring herself to burden him with her troubles, not when he had already been so patient and understanding.

Instead, she mustered a sense of determination, a glimmer of hope flickering within her. "I'll be staying in Raven's Hollow for the next two weeks," she told him. "But I can't wait to see you again when I get home."

There was a brief pause before Jerry responded. His voice was warm and affectionate. "I can't wait to see you too, Evie," he said, his words a silent reassurance of their love.

As Evelyn ended the call, a sense of relief washed over her. Despite her uncertainty of the future between them, she knew that Jerry was there for her. And for that, she was grateful.

With the weight of her conversation with Jerry momentarily lifted, she took a deep breath. The next two weeks would be challenging because she hadn't actively practiced as a therapist for a while. She determined to give it her best, knowing that was all she could do.

Turning away from the phone, she found herself drawn back to the present moment, back to the quiet comfort of the house. She glanced around the room, her gaze lingering on the unfamiliar surroundings, noting the simplicity of it all.

A small desk. An accompanying chair. One window in the room. A throw blanket folded at the foot of the bed. All signs of a lived in space. She turned as she heard footsteps at the door.

Steve approached her. "Everything okay?" he asked, his voice gentle as he reached out a hand to touch her arm.

Evelyn nodded, offering him a grateful smile. "Yeah, everything's fine," she assured him, her voice steady despite the lingering uncertainty of how Jerry truly felt at her departure.

Steve studied her for a moment, his gaze searching hers for any sign of distress. Satisfied with what he saw, he nodded, a silent acknowledgment of her strength. "Good," he said simply, his tone filled with quiet understanding.

He eventually left her and went on his way. In the stillness of the night, the moon cast its ethereal glow through the window of her room. Evelyn found herself drawn to the beauty of it. Seemingly cold, definitely ethereal. Standing before the window, bathed in the soft moonlight, she hesitated, her gaze fixed on the darkness beyond.

With a sigh, Evelyn turned away from the window. She crawled into bed. Reaching for the nightlight on the side table, she hesitated. Her fingers hovered uncertainly over the switch. It seemed foolish, she thought, to be afraid of the dark at her age. But in the quiet solitude of the night, the shadows seemed to dance with a life of their own, whispering secrets that Evelyn couldn't decipher.

In the end, she decided to leave the light on, the soft glow casting a warm and reassuring blanket over the room. It was a small comfort, perhaps, but one that she welcomed nonetheless.

As she settled into bed, the rhythmic pulse of the night surrounding her, Evelyn allowed herself to drift into a restless sleep. In the dead of night, she was jolted awake by the remnants of a haunting nightmare, her heart pounding in her chest as she gasped for breath. Disoriented and drenched in sweat, she struggled to recall the details of the dream that had left her shaken to the core. Blinking away the haze of sleep, she failed to recall and deemed it unimportant. Relegating it to the stress she was under.

Evelyn glanced around the darkened room. Had she left the lights on before she fell asleep? She then remembered waking up once and turning the light off.

With a shaky exhale, Evelyn forced herself to focus. She reached out in search of the comforting glow of the lamp, but stopped. She sat in silence and found solace in the quiet darkness, a sanctuary of stillness.

She lay back, closed her eyes and took a deep, steadying breath. And as the echoes of her nightmare faded into the recesses of her mind, she allowed herself to surrender, the darkness becoming not a threat, but a quiet place where nothing demanding anything from her. A mercy to herself.

Chapter 4

The morning sun gently filtered through the curtains as Jerry stirred awake. He was in his childhood bedroom at his parents' house in the Hamptons. The soft rustle of sheets served as a stark reminder that Evelyn wasn't there.

Jerry rubbed his eyes and sat up with a heavy sigh. His thoughts drifted back to Evelyn. Her dark flowing hair, her once bright eyes—the latter seemed distant now. He'd noticed changes creeping in over the past few months, though he couldn't quite pin down where they'd started.

Ever since she'd left her lucrative practice for academia, something had shifted between them. He couldn't quite put his finger on it, but he knew that Evelyn wasn't as happy as she'd once been.

He moved through his morning routine—showering, brushing his teeth, shaving—but each step felt mechanical, disconnected. Evelyn was withdrawing from their relationship. Not physically. Not wholly emotionally either. Somewhere in between. The subtle changes in her demeanor spoke volumes about whatever she was experiencing.

Yet, despite his concerns, Jerry had hesitated to confront Evelyn about her unhappiness. He'd convinced himself that it was just a minor slump, something she'd eventually overcome with time. But now, as he stood before the mirror, the silence bore down on him.

A breath escaped his lips. He exhaled sharply, straightened his shoulders, and focused on the day ahead. He dressed quickly, the familiar routine of getting ready serving as a temporary distraction.

He made his way downstairs to meet his parents for breakfast, while fully resolving to find a moment to talk to Evelyn later in the day. He knew that he couldn't continue to ignore the growing distance between them. He needed to address the underlying issues that threatened to tear them apart.

But for now, he'd plastered a smile on his face and pushed aside his worries. He'd make the most of the day ahead with his family, even as the unanswered questions continued to bother him.

Breakfast wasn't at home. His parents met him in the foyer. Afterwards, a car was pulled up front and they all entered, headed out to dine.

Amidst the elegant ambiance of the plush restaurant, Jerry sat with his parents, the clinking of cutlery and the soft hum of conversation filled the air around them. His parents were eager to hear about his life in Harrisburg, leaning in with curiosity, they inquired about his work.

"So, how's everything going in Harrisburg? How's work treating you?" asked his mother, Kelly.

With a half-hearted smile, Jerry offered up vague responses, skimming over the intricate details of his scientific endeavors, knowing all too well that the complexities of his research would sail over his parents' heads.

Forcing a smile, Jerry replied, "Oh, you know, the usual. Work keeps me busy."

He appreciated their interest, but concerns for Evelyn loomed large in his mind, overshadowing any enthusiasm he might have mustered for discussing his *own* life.

Martin, Jerry's father, chimed in. "Any exciting projects on the horizon?"

Jerry nodded vaguely. "Yeah, a few things in the pipeline."

"And how's your research coming along? You always were so passionate about it," asked Kelly.

Jerry said, "It's progressing. Slowly but surely. I'm working with some teams to work on the company's main project. They've decided to make me the team lead."

Jerry trailed off. He'd given more of a response this time than any other, but his parents were still sensitive to the disconnect.

Lost in his thoughts, Jerry absentmindedly toyed with the utensils in his hand, his attention drifting away from the conversation at hand. His parents exchanged knowing glances, recognizing the telltale signs of their son's preoccupation. They knew him well enough to sense that something was troubling him, something weighing on his mind.

Martin asked, "Is everything alright, son? You seem a bit preoccupied."

Jerry stopped fiddling with his utensils. His answer was just as vague as his first responses. "Oh, it's nothing, just lost in thought, I guess."

His mother shifted gears, deciding to mention Jerry's best friend, Frank, recently inquiring about him.

"Frank asked about you the other day. He's been wanting to catch up," said Kelly

Jerry seemed to perk up slightly. The mention of Frank briefly sparked some interest in Jerry's eyes. "Frank? That's nice. I'll give him a call later."

Martin said with a smile, "Good idea, son. It's been a while since you two caught up."

Jerry replied, "Yeah, it has." He nodded absently. He promised to reach out to Frank later in the day to assure them he wasn't just giving them lip service.

His attention wandered until his parents brought up Evelyn.

Kelly spoke softly. "And what about Evelyn, dear? How's she doing?"

His facade of disinterest melted away, replaced by a furrow of concern creasing his brow. He paused, setting down his utensils, his appetite suddenly forgotten as he opened up to his parents about his worries regarding her distant behavior.

Jerry hesitated, then finally spoke. "Actually... it's Evelyn. She's been pulling away and I'm worried."

In response, his parents offered words of comfort and advice, reminding him that every relationship had its challenges and that being supportive was key.

"Oh, Jerry, I'm sure everything will be fine. Relationships have their ups and downs," his mother said.

"Just be there for her, son. That's the most important thing," said Martin.

Jerry needed the encouragement. It went a long way to help him gather his thoughts together. "Thanks, Mom, Dad."

Kelly reached across the table and patted her son's hand while giving him a warm smile.

Jerry absorbed their wisdom with a grateful smile. He finally allowed himself to focus on his meal, the conversation shifting to lighter topics.

"Now, let's talk about something more cheerful. Have you heard about our latest trip to the vineyards?" asked his mother.

They delved into discussions about his parents' latest adventures. Jerry was grateful for their support. His worries weren't gone—but for now, they sat quietly at the edge of his mind, content to wait.

Chapter 5

Evelyn stepped into the diner, greeted by the soft murmur of conversation and the clink of utensils on ceramic. The place was busier than she'd expected for a weekday afternoon.

The hostess gave her a sympathetic smile. "Afraid we're packed today. But we do have one open table — though someone else just walked in who might need it too." She nodded toward a woman at the door behind Evelyn.

Evelyn glanced back and met the woman's polite smile.

"Only table left?" the woman asked the hostess.

"Afraid so. You're welcome to share, if you don't mind."

Evelyn hesitated for a moment. The woman didn't seem put off — if anything, she looked amused.

"Fine by me," she said.

"Me too," Evelyn added. "Better than waiting."

They both smiled as they slid into opposite sides of the small booth.

"You look a bit lost. Are you from around here?" asked Evelyn with a wry smile. "It's not like I'm exactly a local either."

The woman's eyes brightened with amusement. "Is it that obvious?" she chuckled. "No, I'm just passing through." She extended her hand across the table. "My name's Jessica Monroe."

Evelyn shook her hand. "Well, it's nice to meet you, Jessica. I'm Evelyn Harper."

"So, you from around here?" Jessica asked.

Evelyn shook her head. "Nope. Not even close."

"I'm spending a little time here. It's... charming." Jessica smiled. "Definitely not what I'm used to."

Evelyn nodded. "Same here. Work brought me in."

They exchanged a few harmless comments about small town quirks—the cozy feel, the slow pace, how everybody seems to know everybody else's business. Their voices blended in easily with ebb and flow of conversations around them. Jessica made a small self-deprecating remark.

"I swear, I walked into one shop and they already knew my name. It's that kind of small town."

Evelyn laughed lightly in response.

A few tables of men glanced in their direction. Evelyn lowered her eyes briefly but caught Jessica noticing too. Jessica spoke up before Evelyn realized that she would.

"I take it you're not used to guys checking you out?"

Evelyn hid her smile behind her menu. The attention from the nearby table reminded her of Jerry and their first meeting. Unlike most men, his gaze never dropped or wandered.

He kept his eyes fixed on hers the whole time, never once letting them drift—not once up and down. He'd look away occasionally but that was it. It wasn't predatory, not invasive. Just... steady. Focused. Like he was genuinely interested in *her*—who she was, not what she looked like. That was what unsettled her. Not his gaze, but her discomfort at being truly seen.

"It's been a bit strange," Evelyn admitted, her voice tinged with uncertainty. "I don't usually pay attention to things like that. I find that since I've been here, however, I'm more sensitive to things like that."

Jessica's eyebrows raised in surprise. "Do you think there's a particular reason you feel that way."

Evelyn didn't immediately answer. She simply met Jessica's eyes.

Jessica raised her hands. "Sorry. Not trying to get personal."

Evelyn shook her head to disarm the slight tension, relieved to have found someone interesting. "No. It's alright. I was surprised by the question, is all.

Jessica smiled.

"I've got things... I'm worried about. Because of that, I've been feeling like an outsider ever since I arrived and I'm noticing a lot of things I normally wouldn't pay attention to."

Jessica's expression softened. "That happens fast in towns like this. You stand out. But honestly, that's not always a bad thing."

"I guess you're right," Evelyn responded. "And by the way, you stand out too. You're quite pretty."

"Thank you," said Jessica.

A moment later, she stretched. "Well, no sense sitting around. If you feel like stretching your legs, we could check out some shops after lunch. What do you say?"

Evelyn's lips curved into a genuine smile, grateful for the offer of companionship. "That actually sounds nice. I'd like that," she replied, her worries momentarily pushed aside by the prospect of newfound friendship.

"The more the merrier, right?" Jessica grinned.

With a shared laugh and a sense of camaraderie, Evelyn and Jessica set off to tour the town after they finished their meal.

As they strolled through the quaint streets, their conversation flowed easily—backgrounds, interests, and experiences, enjoying each other's company.

As they passed by the charming storefronts and cozy cafes, Evelyn felt a sense of relief in Jessica's presence. There was something comforting about talking to someone new, someone who wasn't entangled in the complexities of her work and personal life.

Rather than getting into her professional life, Evelyn let the conversation center on lighter things— her love for art, her passion for travel, and her recent struggles with finding balance in her personal and professional life.

Jessica was a receptive listener, offering words of encouragement and support as Evelyn opened up about her experiences. There was an unspoken understanding between them, a mutual appreciation for the opportunity to connect on a human level, free from the constraints of their respective roles.

In Jessica's company, Evelyn's responsibilities seemed to lift, if only for a moment, allowing her to enjoy the simple pleasures of friendship and companionship.

Chapter 6

After breakfast with his parents, Jerry had reached out to Frank. He felt a twinge of nostalgia for their old friendship. Recalling their past interactions, though, made him realize the reason why he'd slightly distanced himself from a more active role in maintaining their friendship—the discomfort he always felt around him. Frank always seemed a bit... self absorbed. Not maliciously so, just enough that Jerry didn't feel like they *clicked* anymore.

They agreed to meet at a local bar later that evening, a decision Jerry now found himself questioning as he navigated the crowded streets on his way to their rendezvous.

He spotted Frank at a corner table upon entering the dimly lit establishment. Frank's animated gestures drew the attention of nearby patrons—and Jerry. He made his way over, not truly knowing what to expect.

Frank greeted him with a half hug, one arm encircling him while shaking hands with the other. A real smile was spread broadly across his handsome face, making him seem approachable. His friendly nature was real. Not polished. Not performative. Despite that, Jerry braced himself for the possible onslaught of Frank's self-centered banter, unsure of how he would navigate the evening without succumbing to frustration.

The drone of voices combining in the bar provided a backdrop for Frank's dominance, his voice easily drowning out the subdued chatter. Jerry tried to keep up with the animated monologue, but it was a struggle against the tide of Frank's anecdotes.

"Jerry, my man! Good to see you, buddy," Frank exclaimed.

Returning the greeting with a nod, Jerry took a seat across from Frank.

"You're looking good." Frank stated.

"Just keeping busy with work and stuff," Jerry replied, trying to downplay his own accomplishments to avoid sparking Frank's competitive streak.

Frank leaned back in his seat, a smug grin spreading across his face. "Work, huh? Yeah, I've been absolutely killing it at the firm lately. Promotions left and right, you know how it is."

Jerry forced a polite smile.

Frank's eyes gleamed with anticipation, as if eager to share even more.

"So, Jerry, tell me, how's life treating you?" Frank's eyes gleamed with curiosity.

Jerry hesitated, unsure of how to navigate the familiar rhythm. "Well, it's been..." he'd only just begun. He was immediately cut off by Frank's sudden interjection.

"But enough about me, let's talk about you," Frank declared, his tone brimming with faux sincerity. "How's that job of yours? Still slaving away for peanuts?"

Jerry's brows knitted. He wondered if Frank actually cared what he was about to say or was just filling air to hear himself talk. He'd already asked him a similar question before interrupting him.

He sighed inwardly, recognizing the familiar pattern. Redirecting the conversation back to himself, even when asking about someone else. Countless evenings of Frank's self-promotion rushed back. Jerry understood that his own experiences were going to be, once again, relegated to the sidelines.

"It's... fine," Jerry replied, his words tinged with resignation. "But enough about work, how's everything going with you?"

Frank's eyes lit up at the opportunity to talk. He leaned in, flashing his signature grin. "Oh, you know, same old, same old. Closed a seven-figure deal last week. You should've seen their faces when I walked out with that contract. Oh-and finally picked up the AMG S-Class I was eyeing. Handles like a dream."

Jerry lifted his glass to his lips and took a sip while Frank spoke on. His eyes drifted to survey the space. He'd only devoted part of his attention, just enough to pick up the clues for where his "uh huh," and "really," were expected to be inserted in. He felt a pang of nostalgia for the friendship they had once shared. When they were just boys in the neighborhood. Riding bikes. Running around barefoot. Chasing baseballs instead of fame and notice. But beneath the surface, he knew that their bond had been eroded by Frank's relentless pursuit of validation.

Resigned to endure the remainder of the evening, Jerry silently vowed to find a graceful exit from their get-together, his mind already formulating excuses to extricate himself from Frank's company without causing offense.

As the evening wore on, Jerry found himself increasingly uncomfortable with Frank's antics. Frank's eyes lit up when he spotted two women sitting nearby, and before Jerry could protest, Frank had already begun inviting himself, and Jerry, into their sphere.

"Hey ladies, mind if we join you?" His confidence was unwavering as he approached the pair.

With a forced smile, Jerry followed Frank to the women's table, feeling like a reluctant participant.

Bethany and Helen were the girl's names, he'd later find out.

Jerry watched as they smiled warmly at Frank. He shrugged. The guy had always been able to get interest from women. It wasn't the bragging. It was his looks and his very open and unapologetic personality. Jerry laughed lightly, realizing that Frank could be so much more if he was aware of his tendency to seek validation of his accomplishments.

Frank wasted no time in launching into his usual routine, regaling the women with his charm. Jerry found it fascinating how they responded eagerly.

Bethany's eyes widened with interest, a hint of flirtation in her gaze as she nodded eagerly. "Sure, take a seat!" she chirped, scooting over to make room for the newcomers.

Jerry felt like the odd one out as they settled into their seats. That is, until Frank opened his mouth a moment later.

"So Jerry here," Frank announced, gesturing toward Jerry with a flourish, "is a brilliant guy, top of his field. You should hear about the amazing projects he's been working on lately."

Jerry shifted uncomfortably in his seat. Bethany and Helen turned their attention toward him. He managed a weak smile, unsure of how to respond to Frank opening the floor for him. He sighed heavily and told them about his work. They were attentive. Interested. But not overly so. His work was, truth be told, rather boring.

Frank kept setting Jerry up with little openings, drawing him into the conversation. He'd not ignored Jerry in the least and seemed, instead, to promote his own friend. Not that it kept him from promoting himself even more.

He wanted to put an end to his shameless flirting. No. He wanted to put an end to Frank leading the women to believe he was interested in them.

The conversation continued to flow, with Frank dominating the discussion and the two women hanging on his every word. Jerry found himself increasingly disengaged, his mind wandering to thoughts of Evelyn and the comfort of their relationship.

Jerry, eventually, had had enough, his frustration reaching its breaking point. When he finally made the decision to leave, he could feel the disappointment in Bethany and Helen's eyes as they watched him stand.

"Leaving so soon, Jerry?" Frank called out, a hint of confusion in his voice as Jerry rose from the table.

"Yeah, I've got an early start tomorrow," Jerry replied, his tone terse as he gathered his things.

He stood, left a few bills on the table to cover his share, barely acknowledging Frank's bewildered expression as he made his exit.

Outside the bar, he took a deep breath, relief flooding through him as he distanced himself from the chaos. He was disappointed in Frank's behavior but more disappointed in himself. He admonished himself, realizing that their friendship had become nothing more than a series of one-sided conversations and empty gestures.

He walked away from the bar, longing for the comfort and stability of Evelyn's presence. This, despite their current issues. He wished for nothing more than to spend his time with her instead of enduring another evening with others who didn't enrich his life. He longed for the genuine connection he shared with Evelyn.

Chapter 7

In the subdued ambiance of Steve's living room, Evelyn and Steve sat across from each other, their conversation focused on the case they worked together. Steve's brow furrowed in deep contemplation, while Evelyn's features betrayed a mix of concern and discomfort.

"The details the patient shared with me about his childhood... they seem so ordinary, almost mundane."

Steve nodded thoughtfully, rubbing his chin pensively. "I know what you mean. It's normal, so it's hard to pin down what he's dealing with that's causing the nightmares. I don't suspect it's his childhood. It's probably something he's dealing with now that he doesn't have the social tools to handle."

Evelyn shifted in her seat, her mind racing with possibilities. She had hoped that her sessions would provide clarity, but instead, they only seemed to muddy the issue.

"Have you noticed anything else? Any patterns or recurring themes in his stories? The people around him?" Evelyn inquired, trying to glean any insight.

Steve paused, his gaze lingering on Evelyn. "Not really, no. He's guarded, even with me. But there's something about your approach, Evelyn, that seems to resonate with him."

"Well, whatever the case may be, I think we're making progress."

Steve nodded in agreement. "Agreed. I really think you're the key to helping. Maybe he just needed a woman's touch, someone who could empathize with him on a deeper level."

That being said, they wrapped up their session. Evelyn retreated to the solace of her room. She sat on the bed and rubbed her ankle. The events of the day lingered, slowly unfolding. Jessica had been a fun distraction. Her session with Alex had gone as expected. Now, she was left with her thoughts of her own issues. She hadn't contacted Jerry, yet.

Before surrendering to the embrace of sleep, Evelyn found herself drawn once more to the bedroom window, a curiosity compelling her to peer into the darkness beyond. A view of the stars overhead seemed in order. Something to ponder beyond the limitations of her terrestrial existence.

She gazed first at the houses in the neighborhood. Figures were silhouetted against the glow of their illuminated homes as they passed windows. More intent on their internal lives. Evelyn sought to move away from that direction. She didn't *want* to think about internal issues. She stood motionless in the window, her eyes fixing upon the stars overhead. Her gaze held on the stars for a while, lost in the silence.

Evelyn slowly drew the curtains shut, her heart noticeably pulsing in her chest as she retreated to the safety of her bed. The effects of mindfulness. The darkness of the room offered a place of quiet contemplation.

Evelyn reached for her phone, a longing for connection driving her to seek the familiar voice of Jerry. After a few rings, her call was answered.

"Jerry?" she whispered into the phone, her voice tinged with apprehension.

"Yeah, Evie, it's me. Is everything alright?" Jerry's voice, groggy with sleep, offered a brief respite from the encroaching darkness of self doubt. Self questioning. Self recrimination and fear of failure that plagued her so much lately.

Evelyn hesitated, unsure of how to articulate the turmoil swirling within her. "I... I just wanted to hear your voice," she admitted softly.

"Hey, I'm here."

Evelyn smiled. Then she worried about how his voice had greeted her. "Was it too late to call you?"

"You know you can call me anytime, right?" Jerry's reassurance was like a balm to her.

They exchanged banalities, the mundane details of their lives serving as a fragile barrier against the encroaching feeling of separation. Evelyn longed to confide in him, to share the weight of her fears, but a sense of childish embarrassment held her back.

As their conversation drew to a close, Evelyn's heart swelled with love. "I love you, Jerry," she whispered, the words a fragile lifeline in the silent expanse of the night.

But suddenly, the connection faltered, the line falling silent as the phone slipped from Evelyn's grasp. She attempted to call back, only to realize that she had no cell phone service.

Resigned to deal with it in the morning, Evelyn turned in for the evening, disappointed that she couldn't hear Jerry return her gesture of love before the connection died.

The soft hues of dawn filtered through the curtains, rousing Evelyn from her restless slumber. She reached for her phone, noticing a missed call from Jerry, accompanied by a message expressing concern about their interrupted conversation.

Frowning, she dialed his number, relief washing over her when he answered. "Hey, sorry about last night," she began, her voice laced with regret.

"It's okay, Evie. I just wanted to make sure you're alright," Jerry replied, his tone gentle yet tinged with worry.

Evelyn hesitated, her unspoken troubles pressing on her. "I'm fine, Jerry, really," she assured him, though she knew he could sense her reluctance to delve into the true issues.

Jerry's concern was palpable even through the phone line, his words a comforting balm to her troubled mind. "Alright, but don't be a stranger," he said, his voice filled with light mirth. A serious kind of levity that helped to soften his disquietude.

With a grateful smile, Evelyn thanked him before bidding him goodbye, a sense of warmth lingering in her chest as she hung up the phone.

Entering the kitchen, she found Steve already there, a steaming mug of coffee in hand. "Morning," he greeted, his gaze curious yet understanding.

"Hey," Evelyn replied, returning his smile as she poured herself a cup of coffee. "Just had a quick chat with Jerry."

Steve nodded, sipping his coffee thoughtfully. "Glad to hear he got through. Cell service around here can be pretty spotty," he remarked, his tone casual yet tinged with concern.

"You didn't tell me that when I got here," Evelyn said as she retrieved a mug from the cabinet.

"You didn't ask," Steve laughed. "Most of the time though, it doesn't happen. There was a storm a few miles north of here that caused the issue. Somewhere on the other side of the Allegheny forest."

Evelyn nodded like she understood. She hadn't like losing the call with Jerry the night prior but she had no choice but to accept it. It wasn't like it was super important, but she'd minded. She'd wanted to connect. She shrugged her shoulders, reminding herself she wasn't here for much longer before shifting back to the day at hand.

They sat in companionable silence. Evelyn's thoughts drifted to her sessions with Alex. There was another scheduled for the afternoon. She was going to start shifting towards the direction she and Steve had settled on the night previous.

Evelyn finished her coffee and decided to see the town again. Steve joined her. The small size not withstanding. It was quaint and walking the familiar streets still felt fresh and new. The lingering smiles of the townspeople, the laughing of children, and the inexplicable friendly waves she witnessed paradoxically reminded her of what she was missing.

'What's going on here?' she wondered, her mind racing. Is it just me, or is this town telling me to face up to my life?

Evelyn looked over at Steve. "How do you deal with something you don't want to deal with?"

Steve glanced at her, his expression unreadable. "What do you mean?"

"Just asking in general. Being here is peaceful but that peacefulness makes what isn't peaceful stand out more in contrast," Evelyn explained, her voice tinged with apprehension. "It's like it amplifies what's wrong because it feels so right."

Steve shrugged, his tone nonchalant. "Ah, don't worry about it, Evelyn. It's not the town. Probably just a coincidence. I'm not trying to dismiss it. Even I felt that way when I first moved here. But I think it might be because we see something in the quiet that reflects the loud things in our lives and makes them louder in comparison."

But Evelyn wasn't convinced with that answer.

'Did he really believe that? Or is he aware of how lost I really am?'

His response only added to her sense of confusion.

She mused that it might not be the town that made her feel that way. The town was likely more of an external catalyst that *made* her aware of the disconnect. Something that prompted her to turn inward and look. She shook her head, and continued to walk silently beside Steve.

She resolved to stay more aware of her own thoughts, knowing they weren't as quiet as she'd have previously believed. Not as quiet as the world around her.

Chapter 8

Jerry sat on the plush couch in his parents' living room, his recent encounter with Frank still lingering in his mind. He fidgeted with his phone, contemplating whether to call Evelyn or not.

He missed her—her voice, her presence, her comforting embrace. But he also feared what he might hear on the other end of the line. The woman who seemed to be withdrawing. Growing distant and closed off.

With a deep breath, Jerry dialed Evelyn's number, the familiar tones of the ringing phone filling the room. He listened anxiously as the line connected, his heart pounding in his chest.

"Hey, Jerry," Evelyn's voice greeted him, soft and warm, instantly easing some of his tension.

"Hey, Evie," Jerry replied, relief flooding through him at the sound of her voice. "How're you doing?"

There was a moment of hesitation on the other end of the line before Evelyn responded. "I'm okay, Jerry," she said, her tone careful. "Just taking things one day at a time."

Jerry sensed something pointing towards his fears in her words, the underlying turmoil she was trying to conceal. He wanted to reach through the phone and wrap her in his arms, to offer her comfort and support.

But.

He knew he couldn't do that from miles away.

He hesitated, then decided it was time to at least inch towards the one thing that neither of them had named outright, as of yet. "Is everything alright? I mean between us. You've been..." Jerry asked, his concern evident.

Evelyn sighed softly. "It's... complicated. I'm still trying to make sense of things. I'm not trying to run away from..." she admitted, her words trailing off.

"Us?" Jerry offered.

Evelyn didn't speak. She intoned. Jerry heard the, "mm hmm." A positive response? He wasn't sure, but he wasn't going to press.

Jerry felt a pang of frustration and helplessness. He wanted to understand, to help her in any way he could, but it seemed like Evelyn was keeping him at arm's length.

"I'm here, Evie," Jerry said earnestly. "Whatever you're going through, don't do it alone."

There was a pause on the other end of the line, and Jerry held his breath, waiting for Evelyn's response.

"I know you're there, Jerry. I don't want to drag you into my issues..." Evelyn replied, her voice tinged with emotion.

There was a dis-settling quiet before she continued.

"I appreciate that more than you'll ever know. But this is something I need to figure out on my own."

Jerry felt a twinge of disappointment, but he understood. He knew that Evelyn was strong and independent, and he respected her need for space.

"Alright," Jerry said softly, his heart heavy with longing. "Just know that I love you, Evie. And I'll be here whenever you're ready."

"I love you too, Jerry," Evelyn replied, her voice filled with warmth and affection. "More than anything in the world."

They said their goodbyes and ended the call.

Chapter 9

The soft glow of the studio lights cast a warm ambiance over the gathering as Evelyn stepped inside, her gaze scanning the room. The sound of chatter and laughter filled the air, mingling with the subtle clinking of glasses.

She spotted Alex across the room, a charming smile gracing his lips as he engaged in conversation with a group of investors. It struck her as odd, considering the troubles he had confided in her during their therapy sessions.

Making her way through the crowd, Evelyn couldn't ignore the incongruity. She had expected to find Alex in a more subdued state, grappling with the manifestations of his sleep issues, not playing the role of the charismatic host.

As she approached, Jessica caught her eye, her presence equally perplexing. She was effortlessly blending in with the guests, a glass of champagne in hand as she exchanged pleasantries with those around her.

"Evelyn, darling, so glad you could make it!" Jessica exclaimed, her voice dripping with warmth as she embraced Evelyn.

Evelyn returned the hug, her mind racing with questions. "Jessica, what are you doing here?"

Jessica seemed surprised about the query. "What do you mean? I'm Alex's manager."

Evelyn's eyes widened. "Oh. I had no idea."

Jessica chuckled. "Well, when we first met, we didn't exactly go into details about what we did for a living."

Evelyn nodded in agreement. Realizing that fact belatedly.

"So, what is this? What's going on here? I hadn't expected Alex to be hosting..." Evelyn motioned around. A lack of a proper name for what was going on was lost on her for a moment.

"Exhibition?" Jessica offered.

"Yeah. That," said Evelyn.

Jessica smiled, her tone light and casual. "Oh, it was all rather last-minute, I'm afraid. But isn't it exciting? Alex has been working so hard on his latest pieces, it's only fitting that we celebrate his success."

"Now I can understand why you didn't you tell me about this event."

Evelyn's brow furrowed in confusion. She'd been under the impression that today was meant for another therapy session with Alex, not a lavish gathering for investors and admirers.

Jessica caught the hesitation in Evelyn's eyes. In fact, it prompted her to ask her own clarifying questions. "So what are you doing here?"

"I came to see Alex."

"Oh," Jessica intoned.

"I'm here for... professional reasons. He's got things we're working on together."

Jessica didn't say anything. She nodded instead, took Evelyn by the arm gently, and began leading her around the gallery. They moved in silence for a moment, viewing paintings, before Evelyn spoke again.

"I... I think I should go," Evelyn stammered, already feeling the weight of discomfort settling over her.

But Jessica shook her head, her grip on Evelyn's arm not lessening, though not tightening. "Nonsense, darling. You're here now, you might as well enjoy yourself. Besides, Alex would be disappointed if you left so soon."

Evelyn hesitated, unsure whether to stay or leave. In the end, she found herself nodding in reluctant agreement, allowing Jessica to lead her further into the throng of guests.

As the night wore on, Evelyn felt out of place, like a puzzle piece forced into the wrong picture. But for now, she pushed aside her misgivings, plastering on a smile as she mingled with the crowd, all the while wondering what to do about the planned visit to Alex.

Evelyn noted Alex laughing with the investors, his eyes flicking briefly toward Jessica for just a second too long—not enough for anyone else to notice, but she caught it.

She lingered on the periphery of the gathering, observing the lively exchange between Alex and his guests. The art world seemed foreign to her. Beyond her depth or social experiences. She felt out of place. Lost. And this led to her circling thoughts she'd rather avoid.

As Alex spoke passionately about his work, Evelyn's gaze drifted across the room, her attention drawn to him like a magnet. His smile, though warm and inviting, held a hint of something elusive, a flicker of weariness that danced just under the surface.

She realized how different he appeared in this setting, a polished facade masking the vulnerabilities she had glimpsed during their therapy sessions. The same thing that she felt about herself. She recalled the conversations with Jerry. The interactions prior to her leaving to come to Raven's Hollow.

She'd been performing. She hadn't been present. She hadn't been fair to Jerry by withdrawing into herself and leaving him to wonder. Her shoulders hitched. She wiped gently at her cheek and then collected herself quickly.

Despite her reservations, Evelyn remained rooted to the spot, watching as the evening unfolded with an air of detachment. Each time Alex's gaze found hers, she offered a polite smile in return, though beneath the surface, she wondered how he managed.

The night wore on, Evelyn's resolve wavered, and with a final glance at Alex, she made her decision, slipping quietly out of the studio and into the cool night air.

The following day found Evelyn back at the studio. She greeted Alex with a curt nod, her demeanor tinged with a hint of reproach.

"Alex, you were supposed to be resting. Taking it easy," she began, her voice firm yet tinged with uncertainty.

Alex's expression softened, a faint furrow forming between his brows as he regarded her with a mixture of concern and understanding. "I'm sorry, Evelyn. I should have told you about the event, especially knowing you were scheduled to meet with me."

Evelyn nodded, her gaze steady as she met his eyes. "It's not just about the event," she replied, her tone measured. "You seemed... different last night. I could tell you were putting on an act. I could see the struggle to stay attentive to your guests."

A flicker of vulnerability passed over Alex's features, his mask slipping for a moment before he regained his composure. "I know," he admitted, his voice tinged with regret. "I wanted to show you a different side of me, a side that isn't burdened by whatever it is I'm dealing with."

Evelyn's heart softened at his words, a surge of empathy flooding her senses. "I understand," she murmured, reaching out to touch his arm in a gesture of reassurance. "But we need to be honest with each other if we're going to make any progress. You need to be honest with yourself."

Evelyn winced after she realized what she'd said. Her lip slipped between her teeth. *Fair advice. I should take it myself,* she thought.

In the meantime, Alex nodded. "You're right. From now on, I'll make sure to keep you in the loop, and take care of myself."

Chapter 10

As Evelyn stepped into Alex's office, she was met with the sight of Jessica engaged in conversation with him. She hesitated, unsure whether to interrupt their discussion, but Alex's warm smile reassured her.

"Ah, Evelyn, I'm glad you're here," Alex greeted, motioning for her to take a seat. "Just a few more minutes with Jessica, if you don't mind."

Evelyn nodded, masking her slight disappointment with a polite smile. "Of course, take your time," she replied, her voice tinged with a hint of resignation.

Deciding to make the most of the unexpected delay, and the absence of the crowds from the exhibition days earlier, Evelyn wandered through the art gallery, her gaze lingering on Alex's paintings. The series, titled "The Truth of Things," held a mesmerizing quality, each brushstroke capturing the essence of its subject with haunting clarity.

As she studied the paintings, a sense of how uncanny Alex had realistically captured his subjects sent a shiver down her spine. An eerie semblance of reality. Not unsettling in a bad way, but a scariness at the realization of *exactly* how talented this man was.

Alex's voice broke through her reverie, drawing her attention back to the present. She turned to face him, her expression thoughtful.

"I hope you've been enjoying the gallery," he said, his voice tinged with warmth.

"Yes, it's quite... captivating," she replied.

"What do you think about them, though?"

"They're compelling," she admitted, choosing her words carefully.

Evelyn reflected on her earlier thoughts of the town. Quiet. A quiet that made the internal noise all that much louder. That's what Alex's paintings did to her as well and what troubled her about them. They made her interior landscape louder than she wanted.

"They're almost as real as real life. Like they're too real."

Alex's smile faltered for a moment, a shadow passing over his features before he regained his composure. "I understand," he replied, his tone measured. "Art has a way of evoking emotions we may not always be comfortable with."

"Don't get me wrong," said Evelyn defensively. "I didn't mean that in a bad way. It's just that the quiet settings of your works got me thinking about something I'm not ready to... deal with yet." She looked away slowly. Her gaze settling somewhere beyond where they currently were.

Alex had been thinking that she didn't like his works but now, he saw differently. "I think I misunderstood what you were saying," he said softly.

Evelyn shook her head. His words brought her back from that place she'd drifted to. "No, you don't have to apologize. It's my fault for not being clearer."

She turned away and looked around the studio. "Anyway, let's move on. You don't have to worry about me. That's not what I'm here for. I'm here to help you."

Alex nodded. Evelyn noted that he didn't seem as disappointed as earlier. That was a good thing.

She glanced once more at the paintings, a sense of familiarity greeted her, the feeling growing stronger with each passing moment.

Her gaze fixated on the portrait in front of her. A rendition of a little girl. Evelyn leaned in closer, she noticed the effect of the child's eyes follow her. "Wow. You really know how to paint," she muttered under her breath.

Just then, Jessica approached, her presence drawing Evelyn's attention away from the unsettling paintings. "Hey, Evelyn," Jessica said, her smile bright but her eyes betraying a hint of sadness.

"Hi. It's good to see you again," Evelyn responded.

She noted Alex's rapt attention focused on Jessica from the side of her eye before quickly bringing her own attention back to Jessica.

"Same here. Did you want to get together later and have dinner or something. Maybe go out trail walking again later?"

Jessica shook her head. "I'm heading back to Harrisburg later this evening."

"Well here, take my card and contact me anytime," said Evelyn as she slipped a business card into Jessica's hands.

Jessica took it with a smile. "It was nice meeting you. I'll call you soon. Maybe we can get together on a later date."

Evelyn returned the smile. "I'd like that," she replied. As Jessica turned to leave, Evelyn couldn't shake the feeling that she was missing something. Alex was again fixated on her. His smile, melancholy and full of... longing? She wasn't sure.

The expression was fleeting as he watched Jessica depart. It was a subtle, but it spoke volumes, leaving Evelyn with a gnawing sense of a connection she couldn't quite put a finger on. Maybe her departure was more than Alex could handle? He might be heavily dependent on her and not realize it?

As Alex turned his attention back to her, Evelyn pushed aside her roaming thoughts.

His disarming smile graced his features. He beckoned her into his office with an air of charm and confidence. "I'm ready to begin, if you are," he said, gesturing for her to join him in his office.

With a final glance at the paintings, Evelyn followed Alex into his office, her mind buzzing with unanswered questions. But, those questions didn't matter. She shrugged it off.

"Please, have a seat," Alex said, gesturing towards a plush armchair positioned opposite his desk. His voice was smooth, but Evelyn could tell it was a facade. Not practiced. Just hiding exhaustion that carried over into the dark smudges beneath his eyes.

"Do you like Raven's Hollow so far?"

Evelyn hesitated, unsure of how much to reveal. "It's... certainly a unique place," she replied cautiously, choosing her words with care.

Alex chuckled. "That it is," he agreed.

"Why do you ask?"

Alex seemed to pause. He looked out of his office at the front door where Jessica had left.

"Oh, I'm thinking of relocating somewhere else," he said vaguely.

Evelyn forced a polite smile. "Alright. I won't press if you don't want to share."

"Thank you," said Alex, his voice tinged with forced, but suppressed cheerfulness.

Evelyn adjusted in her seat. She couldn't ignore the weariness in his voice.

"Alex, I really think it would be best if you took a break from your work for a while," Evelyn said. "You need to focus on one thing at a time."

But Alex just chuckled, a hollow sound in Evelyn's ear. Devoid of any real mirth.

"I appreciate your concern, Evelyn, I really do," he said, his voice dripping with false sincerity. "But I can't just drop everything. You're here to help me deal with my mental issues, but I have responsibilities, obligations..."

Evelyn shifted in her seat as Alex dismissed her concerns with a wave of his hand. His charming smile, once so disarming, now seemed really forced.

Evelyn bit her lip, resisting the urge to argue further. She could sense the underlying tension in Alex's words, even if he kept his tone light and breezy. It was clear that he wasn't going to budge on this issue, no matter how much she pushed.

"Alright, Alex," she said finally, her voice tinged with resignation. "But I need you to understand that if you're not willing to prioritize your own well-being, then I may not be the right person to help you."

For a moment, there was silence as Alex stared at her with an intensity that made Evelyn unsure if she made the right choice coming back into therapy. Then he said, "I have investors to answer to. I know what's best for me. I won't let anything stop my painting—and I *am* taking care of myself."

What followed was another hour long session. Evelyn got more of a feel of who Alex was. She had some idea of the pressures he faced and gathered the information necessary to start piecing together where his issues began.

As Evelyn left the session, she felt unease. Alex's demeanor had set her on edge. His disregard for his own wellness was unsettling. But for now, all she could do was weigh her options and decide whether to continue down this path or to step back and let someone else take the reins.

As Evelyn stepped out of Alex's studio, she rolled her shoulders and heard a quiet crack. The tension from the session sat heavier than she realized. Something was seriously wrong with Alex. His dismissive attitude had left her concerned with how she was going to help him through these nightmares he was having.

She made her way back to Steve's house, her thoughts swirling in confusion. The streets of Raven's Hollow seemed eerily quiet as she walked, the only sound the echo of her footsteps on the pavement. It was as if the town itself was holding its breath, waiting for permission to live in peace.

She let herself in, went straight to the fridge, and pulled something out. She then sat at the table, fidgeting, unable to keep still.

She shifted to look out the window towards the backyard, glancing at the failing light's last struggle landing on the kitchen floor as evening inevitably approached. She'd already taken up the glass and put it down twice, without drinking. Frustrated, she stared at the glass and sighed.

Choosing to stand up and pace, Evelyn found herself still unable to relax. The events of the day replayed in her mind like a haunting melody, each note tinged with a sense of foreboding. Could she help? Would she fail again? She paced the living room, her steps echoing in the quiet house as she wrestled with her thoughts.

"I need to do something," she muttered to herself, her voice barely above stillness. "I can't just sit here."

As the evening wore on, Evelyn found herself drawn back to the paintings she had seen at Alex's studio. Back to her own thoughts about her past and future. Back to thoughts of Jerry. Putting the doubts aside, she pulled out her laptop and began to research the artist and his work.

Hours later, she was rolling her shoulders again. Steve had even brought her a cup of tea halfway through her work. She'd accepted graciously and he'd left her alone for the rest of the night.

Finally, exhausted and overwhelmed, Evelyn closed her laptop and sank back into the couch. She had no idea what to do next, no clear path forward in the face of such overwhelming uncertainty. Alex wouldn't give up working while she and he worked on his issues.

But one thing was certain: she couldn't turn her back on him. Whatever was happening here, she was determined to help.

That night, she had a restless sleep. More because of her own worries about she and Jerry than anything else. She woke to find the sun partially peeking through the blinds. Landing square upon her face. She grimaced, sat up and shielded her eyes from the light as she stretched.

Recalling her visit to the art gallery the day before, Evelyn's mind drifted back to the paintings she had seen. In particular, she couldn't shake the image of the little girl in one of Alex's pieces, her eyes seeming to follow Evelyn's as she moved through the gallery.

Was it a trick of the light or a figment of her imagination? She had to at least give credit to Alex in his use of perspective. It was an odd phenomenon and one that not many artists had the ability to pull off effectively.

Evelyn had dreamed of that painting. The girl's wide, silent stare caught her breath. She wasn't seeing a painting anymore; she was seeing a hollow kind of waiting she recognized too well from her own sense of lost purpose.

She questioned whether her fixation on the portrait was a reflection of her own view of self or a reminder of someone from the past. Her last client. The one that had caused her to abandon her practice.

Evelyn recalled how, in the dream, her gaze fell on the portrait of a little girl — wide eyes, almost too large for her delicate face. Evelyn froze. The loneliness in those eyes tugged at something deep inside her. Familiar. Not from that space, but from long ago. From herself.

Putting those thoughts aside, she set off to begin the sessions. Evelyn decided to confront Alex about taking a break. She couldn't shake the feeling that he needed it.

Evelyn arrived at the art gallery shortly afterward. With a deep breath, she pushed open the door and stepped inside.

To her surprise, the gallery was bustling with activity. People milled about, admiring Alex's paintings and engaging in lively conversation. Evelyn felt a knot form in her stomach as she scanned the room, searching for Alex's familiar face.

And then she saw him, standing near the back of the gallery, surrounded by a group of admirers. He smiled and laughed, charming them with his easy charisma. But there was something about his smile, something that didn't quite reach his eyes.

Evelyn hesitated for a moment, unsure of how to approach him. But then she squared her shoulders and made her way through the crowd, determined to have her say.

"Alex," she said, when she finally reached him. "We need to talk."

Alex turned to her, his smile faltering for a moment before he quickly regained his composure. "Of course, Evelyn," he said smoothly. "Let's step into my office."

As they made their way through the gallery, Evelyn didn't know what to expect, but she was prepared for anything.

Inside the office, Evelyn wasted no time getting to the point. "Alex, I'm concerned about you," she said, her voice steady despite the turmoil raging inside her. "You need to take a break from your work, at least for a little while. It's not healthy to push yourself like this."

But to her surprise, Alex just laughed. "I appreciate your concern, Evelyn," he said, his voice dripping with sarcasm. "But I know what I'm doing. I have to finish what I started."

Evelyn felt a surge of frustration rising within her. How could he be so stubborn, so blind to the dangers that surrounded him? But before she could respond, Alex continued.

"You see, Evelyn," he said, his voice low and menacing. "I have a mission. A mission to give back to this town what it's owed. And nothing, and no one, is going to stand in my way. This town supported me and I've got to give back."

There was something in his tone, something that sent a shiver of fear through her. She realized then that she was dealing with someone who was likely on a path of self destruction.

But despite her growing sense of unease, Evelyn refused to back down. She had come here to help Alex, and she wasn't about to let him slip through her fingers now.

"Alex," she said, her voice firm. "You need help. You reached out to Steve for that help and he brought me into this to see if we could work things out."

Alex sank into his chair. Evelyn watched his hand run though his hair.

"I know I'm not right. I'm tired. I snap at people sometimes. I'm trying to hold it together. Do my best. But I can't stop working. I can't just shut myself away."

Evelyn sighed. He was right. Shutting himself down and isolating wouldn't help with whatever was bothering him. But, she was also aware that Alex stretching himself too thin wasn't helping either.

Eventually, Alex agreed to slow down, at least. With that concession, Evelyn turned and left the office, leaving Alex alone. She didn't know what the future held, but one thing was certain: she wasn't going to fail another person that depended on her.

Chapter 11

The weight of doubt hung heavy on Evelyn's shoulders as she stepped into Steve's house. She had just left Alex's studio, feeling more unsettled than ever about his case. Something about his symptoms didn't quite add up, and she couldn't shake the feeling that there was more to the story than he was letting on.

Recalling how Alex had glanced at Janice a day earlier, she surmised it might be related to her. It was possible that Alex was working himself too much in order to keep her around. Honestly, Evelyn realized it was a possibility, but without Alex's assertion, it remained an assumption.

As she settled into a chair in the living room, Steve looked up from his book, concern etched into his features. "Hey, you look like you've got the weight of the world on your shoulders. Everything okay?"

Evelyn let out a heavy sigh, running a hand through her hair. "Not really, Steve. I just... I don't know. Alex's case is really starting to get to me. His past doesn't seem to match up with his symptoms, and I'm starting to doubt whether my approach to therapy is the right one."

Steve frowned, setting his book aside and leaning forward in his chair. "What do you mean, it doesn't match up? Isn't that what therapy is all about, digging into someone's past to uncover the root of their issues?"

Evelyn shook her head, her brow furrowing in frustration. "Normally, yes. But with Alex, it's different. His past trauma doesn't seem to be the driving force behind his symptoms. It's like there's something else going on. He refuses to back off of work. I can't quite put my finger on it."

Steve nodded thoughtfully, considering her words. "Well, what are you going to do about it? You can't just ignore your instincts. If you think something's not right, you owe it to yourself and to Alex to figure out what it is."

Evelyn chewed on her lip, lost in thought. She knew Steve was right, but doubt that gnawed at her from within. "I don't know, Steve. I just feel like I'm in over my head with this one. Maybe I'm not cut out for this line of work after all."

Her thoughts were circling back to her perceived failures. She thought of Jerry. Her mind navigated back to the troubled young woman she felt she'd failed.

Steve reached out and placed a comforting hand on her shoulder. "Hey now, don't talk like that. You're one of the best therapists I know. You just need to trust yourself and your instincts. You'll figure it out, I'm sure of it."

Evelyn managed a weak smile, grateful for Steve's unwavering support. "Thanks, Steve. I appreciate it. I just wish I had more clarity about what to do next."

Just then, Steve's expression grew somber, his gaze dropping to his hands in his lap. "You know, I've been thinking about something. About your past, and... well, about that patient of yours."

Evelyn's hand clenched her chest at the mention of her past, the memories flooding back with painful clarity. She had tried so hard to bury them, to forget the horror of what had happened. But no matter how hard she tried, the guilt and the shame always seemed to find a way back to the surface.

"I don't want to talk about it, Steve," she said, her voice barely above a whisper. "Please, just... let it go."

But Steve shook his head, his gaze unwavering. "I can't. Not when I see how much it's still affecting you. You blame yourself for what happened, don't you? You think you could have done something to prevent it."

Evelyn swallowed hard. She felt a lump in her throat, tears pricking at the corners of her eyes. She'd spent countless nights agonizing over what she could've done differently, replaying the events of that fateful day in her mind over and over again.

"It's my fault, Steve," she whispered, her voice barely audible. "I should have seen the signs, I should have known she was a danger to herself and others. I failed her, and now... now three innocent lives are gone because of me."

Steve's heart ached as he watched Evelyn crumble before him, her pain etched into every line of her face. He reached out and took her hand in his, squeezing it gently in a silent gesture of comfort.

"It wasn't your fault," he said, his voice soft but firm. "You did everything you could to help her. Sometimes, no matter how hard we try, we can't save everyone."

Quiet settled over the room. The soft tick of a clock close by resounded in the silence. Steve had shifted closer to Evelyn. "It also means we don't have to bear that pain alone."

Evelyn wiped away her tears, her gaze meeting Steve's with a mixture of gratitude and sorrow. "Thank you, Steve. I needed to hear that."

Steve smiled, hope flickering in his eyes. "Anytime."

She'd said that, but hadn't felt it. She hadn't internalized that feeling. There was still something missing.

The image of her former patient flickered in her mind—hollow eyes pleading for help she hadn't been able to give. The failure still bothered her. She had failed to see the warning signs and in the aftermath, she had been left broken with no confidence.

It was a moment that had shattered her illusions of invincibility. She had retreated into the safety of academia, seeking solace in the pursuit of knowledge, desperate to escape the haunting echoes of her past.

But no matter how far she ran, the feeling of failure festered. And now, as she lay in the darkness of her room, she couldn't escape the truth any longer.

Her past left her haunted by the ghost of *inadequacy*. And, as she confronted the demons that lurked within her own mind, she knew that she could no longer hide from the truth.

With a heavy heart, Evelyn acknowledged the pain and the guilt. But she also recognized the strength that had emerged from the ashes of her despair, the resilience that had allowed her to continue moving forward in academia instead.

She sat, staring silently into the cup she held. A feeling of something touching her shoulder passed over her. She looked up and saw Steve still regarding her. It was his eyes taking her in that caused her to feel the touch. His look was... not judgmental. Not pitying. Not cold. Something more real. She could feel the weight of his concern pressing down on her. His furrowed brow and gentle eyes spoke volumes, conveying the depth of his worry without a single word needing to be spoken.

"Evelyn," Steve began, his voice soft but tinged with apprehension, "Your past... It's a heavy burden to bear, but that doesn't mean you stop trying."

Evelyn swallowed hard. She knew Steve was right to be worried. She couldn't let her past dictate her future, but she had. Now, however, she had a job to do, a patient to help, and she couldn't afford to let her own demons get in the way.

"I know, Steve," she replied, her voice steady despite the turmoil churning inside her.

Steve nodded, his expression softening with understanding. "I know you won't. But if you ever feel like it's too much, like you're not able to give him the help he needs, you have to promise me that you'll let me know."

Evelyn met Steve's gaze, a flicker of uncertainty dancing in her eyes. She knew he was right, but the thought of admitting defeat was a bitter pill to swallow. Still, she knew she couldn't ignore his advice.

"I promise, Steve," she said, her voice barely above a whisper. "If I ever feel like I'm not able to give him the care he needs, I'll tell you."

Steve reached out and squeezed her hand in a silent gesture of support, his eyes filled with warmth and reassurance. "That's all I ask. Just take care of yourself, okay? You're important too."

Evelyn managed a weak smile, grateful for Steve's unwavering support. "Thank you, Steve. I'll do my best."

As they sat together in the quiet of the living room, Evelyn felt a sense of relief wash over her. Steve was there to help if she needed it.

And as she drifted off to sleep that night, she knew that no matter what the future held, she wouldn't have to face it alone.

As Evelyn lay in bed, the events of the past dragged like an anchor pulling her down into the depths of despair. She closed her eyes, but sleep eluded her, her thoughts swirling in a tumultuous whirlwind of memories and regrets.

The morning sun cast its warm glow over the quiet streets as Evelyn stepped out onto the porch. She took a deep breath, trying to calm the turmoil churning within her. She'd been stewing inside since the night previous.

She'd made her decision: Alex needed to fully commit, or she couldn't help him. Alex hadn't reassured her of that. She decided that she needed to let Steve know so he'd understand.

Inside the house, Steve's footsteps echoed in the hallway. She met him in the kitchen as he was preparing a small breakfast.

"Look, Steve," she began. "I've been thinking. I'm putting in full effort for this, but I've got to let you know. If he doesn't participate fully, I'm pulling out completely."

It was the only way she could feel safe—take care of her own mental health. She had to put down clear boundaries.

Steve stopped scrambling the eggs he'd been cooking. A slight smell of burnt food emanated from the pan before he absently pulled it off the burner and placed the frying pan on an unlit eye.

Evelyn could sense his frustration building with each passing moment, his anger simmering just beneath the surface like a volcano on the verge of eruption. She moved back.

She felt like she'd made the right choice. She couldn't understand why Steve would seem to be getting angry. Her decision was logical. If Alex continued to refuse to back off of his work, she was going to have to cancel her treatment. It was that simple.

With Alex having given her the impression that he might not seriously commit to taking things slower, she felt the potential for a misconnection between the two that would disrupt the treatment goals. Without Alex's full cooperation, it would be impossible to help him.

Steve's brow furrowed with disappointment. "I can't believe you're just going to walk away like this," he spat, his voice tinged with bitterness. "After everything we've been through, after everything I've done to help you, you're just going to abandon me? I brought you in because you're an expert."

Evelyn's eyes widened. She knew it was the right thing to do. She couldn't continue to treat a patient who refused to listen to her advice, no matter how much she wanted to help.

"I'm not abandoning you, Steve," she said softly, trying to keep her own emotions in check. "I just can't continue to treat Alex if he's not willing to work with me. It's not fair to either of us."

Steve's eyes flashed with anger, his fists clenched at his sides. "Not fair?" he spat, his voice rising with each word. "You think it's not fair? What about me, Evelyn? What about everything I've sacrificed to bring you here, to help Alex? Do you think that's fair?"

Evelyn recoiled at the intensity of Steve's words. They struck her like a slap. She had never seen him like this before, so consumed by frustration. It was as if he had become a different person, a stranger standing before her in the dim light of the hallway.

"I didn't ask you to do any of this, Steve," she said, her voice trembling with emotion. "I came here to help, to do my job. But I can't do that if Alex won't listen to me. I can't force him to change if he's not willing to try."

Steve sighed. His hand moved to his forehead and he rubbed vigorously.

"You're just like all the rest," he said softly, his voice thick with bitterness. "Just another therapist who thinks they know what's best for everyone else. Well, you know what? Maybe you should just leave."

Evelyn's heart sank at the harshness of Steve's words, the sting of rejection cutting deep. "I never intended to say I'd leave. I was meaning I'd back off as the primary. I'd let you take the lead and offer support."

Steve waved dismissively as he turned back to the stove. He put the frying pan back on the flames. "I admit I'm not as good as you. I've only studied general therapy. I can't do what you can do. Even if you support me from the back."

A moment of silence followed. Steve seemed to be done cooking. He turned off the stove and fixed a plate with the food he'd prepared. "If you can't be the primary, then don't worry about it. Just go back."

With a heavy sigh, Evelyn turned and walked out the door, her footsteps echoing loudly in the stillness of the morning. She didn't know where she was going, didn't know what would happen next. But she knew one thing for certain—she couldn't stay in a place where she wasn't wanted.

She got in her car. As she drove aimlessly through the winding streets, her mind rummaged through thoughts of what had just happened.

Was there more to his anger than met the eye. She shook her head. No need in trying to try and figure out someone's intent. She'd never see things the way another person would. It was one of the problems with being human. Being too tied to your own ego didn't allow you to see things from the other person's point of view. Even empathy couldn't help that.

For now, all she could do was drive, her mind consumed. And as the miles stretched out before her, she knew that she couldn't turn back and go home, couldn't retreat into the safety of the familiar. Jerry wasn't there. She had things to do, despite Steve thinking she'd given up. She had to press on.

She drove down a long stretch of road. Suddenly, a figure caught her eye - a lone silhouette walking along the side of the road. Squinting against the glare of the sun, she recognized the unmistakable form of a little girl.

A question passed through her mind. How could a child be out here, alone, in the middle of nowhere?

Slowing down, Evelyn drew closer. The girl appeared to be wearing a pale blue dress. Something that seemed dated. Almost from her own childhood. It wasn't unsettling, just unexpected. She questioned if the child was lost.

As she passed the girl, Evelyn stole a glance. The child's features blurred, her face obscured, then cleared. It was as if she was looking at a specter from the past. The little girl resembled her from in her teens.

Evelyn passed, slowed further, and pulled over. When she got out of the car, she looked back. There was no one there. She leaned against the side of the car and pressed her palms to her forehead.

"I'm projecting. I'm feeling lost so I'm seeing a lost little girl on the side of the road."

She sighed heavily, looked up at the sky, shielding her eyes from the rays of the sun and took a deep breath.

"I need to stop stressing myself out."

A flicker of recognition ignited within her, a memory dredged up from the depths of her subconscious. The girl... the reflection of herself. She remembered being lost as a child. Her father finally finding her hours later. She'd felt so unsure of what to do next. Much like she felt now.

Evelyn continued down the road, leaving the enigmatic girl behind in her memories, where she'd actually been. The encounter left her consumed by the events that seemed to plague her at every turn. Mainly, how she felt about her connections with others.

As Evelyn drove further down the road, in the silence of her car, she glanced in the rearview mirror. She laughed lightly to herself.

"I wanna talk to Jerry," she said softly.

Chapter 12

The bell above the door chimed as Jerry stepped into the cozy coffee shop. The aroma of freshly brewed coffee wafted out. He scanned the room and spotted a familiar face in the corner.

"Neil?" Jerry's voice carried, drawing the attention of his old college friend.

Neil looked up from his laptop, a wide grin spreading across his face. "Jerry! I can't believe it's you!" He rose from his seat, crossing the room to greet him with a firm handshake and a pat on the back.

"Yeah, it's been too long, man," Jerry replied, matching his smile.

They exchanged pleasantries and settled at the table Neil had just left, slipping easily into the rhythm of old friends catching up. The years melted away as they shared updates and reminisced.

"So, how's Ev?" Neil asked, leaning in slightly. A hint of mischief sparked in his eyes.

Jerry's smile faltered. His thoughts drifted to the distance that had grown between them in recent weeks.

"Not great, to be honest," Jerry admitted. "We've hit a rough patch."

Neil raised an eyebrow. "Oh? What's going on?"

Jerry hesitated, brow furrowing as he weighed how much to say. But as he met Neil's steady gaze, he found himself opening up. The words spilled out before he could stop them.

"It's just... Evie's been distant lately. I can't shake the feeling that she's... pulling away from me. I don't know why."

Neil listened intently. He nodded as he processed the words. Then he leaned back in his chair and crossed his arms.

"Well, I can see that happening after that incident with her patient," Neil began, his voice softening.

Neil's tone grew quieter. "You know, she never really talked about it much. But it was pretty serious, what happened with that patient a while back."

Jerry's stomach tightened. He frowned. "I know she left private practice... but she never told me much about why." He sat back, processing. A faint knot twisted in his chest. "I tried to ask once. She always brushed it off. Said she needed a fresh start, that's all."

"I think it was more than that." Neil said gently. She blamed herself, man. From what I heard, someone got hurt. Maybe worse. She never really got past it."

Jerry's eyes widened.

Evelyn's career change—her refusal to talk—weren't just vague personal choices. They were cover. Deflections.

Lies dressed up as protection.

A rush of emotions flooded through him.

He half rose from his seat. "Why the hell didn't you tell me about any of this?" Jerry fumed. His voice was rising enough to bring attention from other patrons in the coffee shop.

Neil glanced at him carefully. "Well... it wasn't my place to say anything. I figured she'd have told you by now."

Jerry still seemed incensed.

"Calm down. Damn," he hissed, reaching across the table and gripping Jerry's forearm.

He waited for Jerry to sit down, take a breath and visibly relax.

"Did she ever talk to you about all of this?" Jerry finally asked.

Neil shook his head. "Naw. I'm just guessing. Putting the pieces together."

"Why would she go through this and not talk to me?" Jerry asked, not really expecting an answer.

He glanced across the table and watched Neil's shoulders rise and fall.

"I don't know, man. I wouldn't even know how to answer that. You've gotta talk to her about that," Neil replied. "It ain't my place to talk about your relationship with Ev. I know we're close but... that's outta my comfort range. Besides, I thought you knew."

Jerry dropped his head into his hands. "I didn't. I had no clue."

A moment of quiet passed. The others in the shop returned to their own conversations by the time Jerry uttered another word.

"I... I had no..." Jerry stammered and trailed off.

"She should have... she would have... told me..."

But even as the words left him, he knew it was a lie. A hollow comfort that couldn't hold against the truth, not even for a breath.

His voice was barely a whisper as he struggled to find the words. Anger, confusion, and a profound sense of sadness swirled within him, threatening to overwhelm him.

Neil offered him a sympathetic smile, reaching out to place a reassuring hand on his shoulder.

"Now you know," he said gently.

Neil paused, letting the words settle. "I know it's a lot to take in, Jerry. But Ev's been through hell, and she's been trying to keep it together, man."

Jerry felt a surge of guilt. He had known Evelyn for four years, had shared so much with her, and yet he had never truly understood the depth of her pain. He had been too wrapped up in his own world, too blind to see the suffering that she carried with her every day.

"Why didn't she tell me?" Jerry whispered again, his voice tinged with bitterness as he struggled to contain his emotions. "Why didn't she trust me enough to share this with me?"

"It ain't easy for her, Jerry. She's been carrying this for years—since before you even met her."

Jerry's anger flared, directed not at Evelyn, but at himself. How could he have been so blind, so oblivious to the pain that Evelyn had been silently bearing? He felt a deep sense of regret wash over him, wishing he could turn back time and be there for her when she needed him most.

"I have to go find her," Jerry declared as he rose from his seat. "I have to make things right."

Neil nodded, seeing the shift in Jerry's eyes.

"Go," he urged. "Go find her and let her know you're there for her."

With a quick nod of gratitude, Jerry left the coffee shop. The only thoughts in his mind: Find Evelyn. Be beside her. Stay beside her.

He climbed into his car and started toward Raven's Hollow.

Chapter 13

The studio door creaked as Evelyn stepped inside.

The heavy scent of paint and stale coffee clung to the air. She spotted Alex across the room, hunched over his canvas, brush in hand, utterly absorbed.

Her stomach twisted.

"Alex," she called sharply.

He didn't respond.

"Alex!" she snapped louder.

He flinched, startled, finally turning toward her. "Evelyn—"

"What are you doing?" she demanded, stepping forward. "We agreed—no work this week. You promised you'd take time off."

His expression tightened. "I'm fine. It helps me clear my head."

"That's bullshit!" Her voice was sharp. She couldn't pull back from the anger coiled inside her.

She didn't know if it was the fear of failure. The idea that this town and his paintings made her think of things she'd rather forget or what. All she knew was, this man hadn't taken her advice even after asking for her help.

"You are exhausting yourself. You're sabotaging any progress we've made," she fired off.

Alex sat down his pallet. He turned and stood off the stool he sat on. He'd crossed half his studio, on his way to a sink to wash his hands, when he said softly, "I said I'm fine. Just let it go."

Evelyn could hear the exhaustion rolling off of him. His voice came like the last vestige of an echo from a distant buried cave.

"You are not fine!" she snapped, her voice rising.

She flung out her hands, waving them aimlessly.

"Every time we talk, you nod, you smile, you pretend to listen, and then you come right back here and bury yourself again. This isn't therapy, Alex. This is self-destruction!"

He turned from the sink, facing her finally. "I'm not self-destructing!" His voice finally cracked. "You don't understand."

"Then help me understand!" she shot back. "Because right now, it feels like you don't want to be helped."

He threw the towel he'd been using to dry his hands down on the table, breathing heavier now.

"I can't stop working!"

Her fists clenched at her sides. "Why? Why the fuck can't you stop? You're not making sense to me."

Alex's shoulders tensed. His eyes darted toward the large portrait of Jessica leaning against the far wall. Evelyn's eyes followed.

"I can't stop working..." he repeated, softer, almost to himself. Then louder—raw, exasperated:

"If I stop working... then I don't have a reason to see her anymore!"

The room froze.

Evelyn stared, stunned. The words echoed in her mind, reframing everything at once.

Her voice dropped. "Her... meaning Jessica." She looked over at the portrait again.

Alex's eyes closed as the admission fully left his lips. There was no taking it back.

Evelyn exhaled slowly. Her anger ebbed — replaced by a sharp, quiet clarity.

Evelyn brushed her hand through her hair. "That's what this is," she said softly. "You're terrified if you don't keep producing, she won't come around."

Evelyn looked around. Spotting a nearby chair she sat heavily.

"She's your manager. Why wouldn't you be able to see her anymore?"

Alex swallowed but didn't speak.

"Why would you tie your work to her?"

"I don't have another way to give her a reason to come see me," he whispered.

Evelyn shook her head. "You're trapped in a cycle you don't know how to break."

He looked like he might argue, but his shoulders slumped. He knew it. She knew it.

Evelyn's voice softened as the tension drained.

"There's gotta be more to this, Alex. Talk to me."

Alex didn't speak. He didn't move. He stood there some minutes before finally shuffling over to a chair near her.

"I love her, that's why."

Evelyn sighed. "Then tell her."

Alex looked at her—wide eyed, mouth hung open. "If I do that... I might change our relationship. What if she doesn't feel the same way? It wouldn't be fair to her to keep managing a guy she rejected. She might feel... uncomfortable."

"You came to therapy for nightmares, Alex. But you weren't dreaming about failure. You were dreaming about losing her. That's what's been chasing you."

Alex looked down at the floor. He rubbed at his face. "I didn't even realize—" his voice broke. "I thought... as long as I kept busy, kept her involved..."

"But the cost is killing you."

He nodded once, small and defeated.

Evelyn sat back, allowing space between them again. Her voice steadied, gentle now.

"Then maybe it's time you talk to her about what you want. Not to me. Not through your work. To her."

Alex said nothing. But for the first time, he looked truly still.

Evelyn offered a faint, tired smile.

"We're done here," she said softly.

She stood and stepped closer to Alex, placing her hand gently on his shoulder. "You didn't need therapy, you needed advice. You needed courage to face..." she trailed off.

The quiet returned. And with it, her realization of how the quiet of Raven's Hollow made her own worries that much louder.

And she turned and left him sitting in the quiet.

Chapter 14

The winding roads curled through open fields and quiet forest as Jerry drove, the afternoon light slipping low on the horizon. He kept one hand loose on the wheel, the other resting absently near the gearshift. The scenery barely registered.

His mind was with Evelyn.

Four years together, and still there were corners of her life he hadn't seen. Not because he hadn't wanted to—but because she hadn't let him. Not fully. Until now.

He hadn't realized how much weight she carried. Not until Neil laid it bare. The pain she kept locked behind soft smiles and careful silence. The way she'd tried to shield him from the pieces of her she was ashamed to show.

He sighed. Maybe he'd done the same in his own way. Staying too careful. Never asking too much. Hoping it would all work itself out.

But love wasn't just about being there when things were easy. It was standing in the heaviness, too. Even when you didn't know how to carry it.

The trees blurred past in streaks of green and gold. The tires hummed steadily beneath him.

He didn't know what he would say when he saw her. Maybe nothing needed to be said. Maybe he just needed to be there. Fully. Finally.

The miles slipped away. The road narrowed. Somewhere just ahead was Raven's Hollow, and beyond that, Evelyn.

Jerry adjusted his grip on the wheel. He exhaled. This wasn't about fixing her. Or fixing anything.

It was simply about arriving.

Chapter 15

The studio door closed behind her with a soft click.

Evelyn paused just outside, letting the cool air wash over her. For the first time in what felt like years, her chest didn't feel tight. She drew in a slow breath, eyes drifting up to the pale sky above Raven's Hollow. The quiet wrapped around her—not heavy, not haunting. Simply... still.

She had helped. Not by overthinking. Not by retreating. Just by being present.

Her hand slipped into her pocket and pulled out her phone. She unlocked it with a swipe and scrolled down through the contacts until she reached Jerry's name.

Her thumb hovered.

For a brief second, her lips curled into a faint smile. A softness.

She tapped the screen and lifted the phone to her ear.

The call failed to connect.

The smile didn't falter.

Of course. Quiet, beautiful, scenic town, but—the reception out here was terrible.

Evelyn lowered the phone and slipped it back into her pocket. She exhaled once, slow and steady, before turning and heading towards her car. Her destination was back to Steve's house.

The small living room was quiet except for the occasional creak of the old floorboards.

Steve handed her a cup of tea as he settled into the chair across from her.

Evelyn wrapped her hands around the warm ceramic, staring down into the swirling liquid.

"I figured out what was bothering Alex," she began.

Steve waited patiently for her to continue.

"Long story short. Love."

Steve let out a humph and shook his head. "Should I ask for details?"

Evelyn laughed gently. Then she recounted the events from the last visit. Steve listened attentively. At some point, he'd broken out a pen and pad and was marking notes. Likely to add to his notes for his client's case. When she was done, Evelyn put down her cup, leaned back into the sofa and sat in silence.

Eventually, she broke the quiet.

A long sigh escaped her lips. She leaned forward, resting her elbows on her knees.

"I was wrong," she said softly.

Steve said nothing, waiting.

"I thought I couldn't do this anymore," she continued. "That I wasn't strong enough. That... I didn't deserve to help anyone." She glanced up, meeting Steve's gaze. "But today—I stayed. I stayed with him, Steve. And it worked. Not because I forced it. Not because I knew everything. Just... because I stayed."

Steve's smile was faint, but steady. "That's the whole thing, isn't it?"

A breath of silence passed.

"You know I brought you here on purpose, right?" Steve asked.

Evelyn's head dropped as a smile crept on her face. "You're an ass, Steve." She finally looked up.

"But," she began softly. "Thank you."

Steve smiled.

"You should fix this issue with Jerry."

She gave a tiny nod. "I see now how much I've been shutting him out. I was so afraid of failing again, I didn't even give him the chance to stand with me."

Steve's eyes softened. "Maybe you're not as broken as you thought."

The words landed gently.

Evelyn's eyes glistened—not with tears, but with something lighter. She smiled, small but true, and nodded once more.

The late afternoon sun dipped lower. The shadows crept across the floor of the living room between them. In the quiet, they heard a car pull into the driveway.

Stepping outside, Evelyn held her arms close to her chest.

The houses of Raven's Hollow sat quietly in her view, quiet and still under the golden light.

The car rolled forward and eased into place. The headlights then flicked off as the engine died.

Waiting on the front porch, Evelyn stood still.

Jerry stepped out of the car.

Their eyes met. She smiled. Jerry exhaled—and smiled back.

No words needed.

They were here.

It is What it is

A low drone filled the room. The result of several fans running at the same time. The sun filtered through unobstructed windows, piercing mercilessly as it crawled across the wooden floor.

Two different sighs resounded, almost one atop the other.

Bob and Frank were stretched out on the sofa. Shirtless. Pant-less if they could have gotten away with it but they couldn't. The sounds of thuds from the ceiling reminded them that their children were at play upstairs.

Bob looked over at Frank. Weary. The day hadn't even progressed toward noon yet. Sweat poured off of their bodies.

"Man, I'm so hot. I'm sweating so much it feels like I'm swimming," said Bob.

Frank didn't even move to indicate he'd heard what was said. However, he did speak. "I'm sweating so much it feels like my eyebrows are drowning."

Silence gathered between them. The fans kept spinning.

"I'm sweating so bad it feels like the bottom of my feet are slippery," said Bob.

Frank laughed lightly. He regretted it right afterwards. Even that seemed to require energy he didn't have.

"I'm sweating so bad, I'm sure the fire department could use the sweat to put out fires," he finally said.

"I'm sweating so bad, my eyelids feel like they're sweating," Bob grinned. He was determined to win this nonsensical competition of who was worse off.

"I'm sweating so bad..." Frank started. His voice drifted off. A moment later, he broke the pause. "I'm sweating so bad it feels like my sweat glands are gonna go on strike, leave, and take a vacation from the heat."

Bob looked over. He leaned forward.

Without a word, he stood, walked to the kitchen and a moment later returned with a full glass of water. He stood in front of Frank and emptied it over his head.

Frank barely responded with movement, but he did ask, slowly, "what was that for?"

"I think your sweat glands did go on strike," Bob replied. "You looked dry as a bone."

After a moment of looking at Frank, he sat down and sprawled out on the couch again.

"Thanks," came Frank's voice floating over the drone of the fans.

"Welcome."

The clock tried to let itself be known by ticking. It could barely be heard. Thuds crossed the ceiling from their right to left. Moments later, to be followed in the opposing direction. Their eyes tracked the dust from the drywall on the ceiling drifting in front of the fan, only to blow away.

"Man, it's so hot, it feels like the room is melting," said Frank, closing his eyes.

"Dude, it's so damn hot," Bob muttered. "Winter feels like a conspiracy theory."

...

Bob groaned softly. Too hot to make it any louder.

Thudding across the ceiling had both their eyes chasing the sound.

"That dude said he'd charge $1500," said Frank softly.

A beat.

"Which do you think hurts less, suffering in this heat or giving out $1500?" asked Bob.

The refrigerator hummed to life in the kitchen.

"What if I give you half?" asked Bob, turning his head slightly to look at Frank from the corner of his eyes.

Frank only responded with a grunt.

Bob started—he really did—to reach for his wallet. His hand fell to the side halfway through the motion.

"Fuck it," he mumbled.

The clock striking 12 finally got through the noise of the multiple fans.

"Damn it's hot..." Bob finally muttered.

"Yeah," Frank whispered.

Holding On

Chapter 1

There was a flicker—subtle, like candlelight at the edge of a mirror—and it danced across her lips before it bloomed into a full smile.

Leland felt the pull of that smile like gravity. It lit her face with a warmth that broke through the dark. Except... *'why was it so dark?'*

The question drifted through his mind like smoke. But the answer didn't matter. Not here. Not now. Not when she was with him.

Helen's fingers laced through his. They stood together, still, grounded in a moment suspended somewhere between memory and dream. The world around them was dim—*'was it night? Or simply absence?'*

Time seemed to hush itself in her presence.

Then came the crack. Sharp. Sudden.

Sound snapped back into existence like a bone breaking. His heart lurched, the silence he hadn't known he was holding splintering into shards. He turned, searching for the source. But the sidewalk, the air, the sky—it all collapsed into one still image.

Helen was no longer standing.

He knelt beside her.

She was in his arms now.

Her body was weightless in a way that made no sense. Head cradled in his lap, her breath shallow. His hands shook as they pressed to her stomach. Warmth spilled between his fingers—not blood, not exactly. Not in the dream. It was light. Blazing, terrifying light that poured from the wound like something sacred being lost.

He tried to hold her together. Tried to push it back in. But it kept spilling out.

"No...oh no..."

His voice sounded foreign. Small. Like it belonged to someone else entirely.

The colors around him twisted. Sky, pavement, skin, hair—all bleeding into one deep, impossibly rich hue. Red. Her red. The red of her hair, her face, her blood, her absence. It painted the world in mourning.

Strangers gathered, their eyes wide and hollow. They said nothing. Could do nothing. Just witnesses to a grief too large for words.

5:45 a.m.

Leland awoke with a violent start. He swallowed the scream lodged in his throat, lips dry and cracking.

He swallowed the scream before it found air.

No use giving it shape. The house was still asleep. And besides, he was tired of hearing it too.

His breath caught in his chest, and it took him a full moment to remember how to breathe. The dream clung to him like wet sheets—sticky, suffocating.

The room came into focus slowly. Dim light. Familiar walls. Real air. He blinked the vision away, forcing the past to retreat.

The ceiling stared back, as it always did—blank stubborn, unwilling to change. He turned.

The red digits on the clock read 5:45 a.m.

Of course it did.

Because?

'Why wouldn't it?'

He hadn't set an alarm in six months. He didn't need to. His body had learned the rhythm of grief—it always woke before the day did. Movement caught his eye.

A figure stood in the doorway.

Angelina. His eldest.

Her silhouette framed by the soft glow of the hallway light. Dark fingernail polish. Thick mascara. Black lipstick that made her mouth look drawn on in ink. Wearing a night shirt with some cute animal in bold colors printed on the front.

She didn't speak right away.

"You were crying out in your sleep," she finally said. Flat. Factual. Not unkind. But not gentle, either.

Leland stared at her, stunned. For a moment, her blue eyes—Helen's eyes—softened. Then she saw that he'd noticed. Her expression hardened like armor.

Her arms crossed.

That same posture. The same sharp defensive stance her mother used to take when a line had been crossed. She didn't know how much she mirrored Helen in moments like these. Or maybe she did. Maybe that's why she used it.

'What was she so angry about though?'

He wanted to ask. But didn't.

She lingered just long enough to make sure he was truly awake, then turned and walked away, her presence evaporating down the hallway.

Leland was left with the stillness. The hum of the air. The ghost of the dream tightening around his ribs like wire.

He lowered his face into his hands. Helen's memory still burned in the space behind his eyes—raw, unfiltered, as sharp now as the day it happened.

'Grief', he thought, *'is never truly silent.'*

'*It waits. Patient. Hidden in the folds of sleep. And when it returns, it spake in screams.*'

He sat there, eyes open, unable to move.

The light on the ceiling changed—barely. But enough to mean morning had begun.

Chapter 2

6:00 a.m.

Leland hadn't moved since Angelina left his doorway.

The weight of the dream clung to him—Helen's warmth fading, her bloodless light spilling through his hands, that unbearable silence cracked open by a scream. He could still feel her fingers in his. Still see the look on Angelina's face when she saw him wake.

The red digits on the clock glared. It didn't care that he felt a need for more sleep his body would never allow.

The bed creaked as he sat up. His joints ached like they were made of rust. He blinked at the window, where a sliver of light tried to peek through the curtains like an uninvited guest.

A breeze moved through the curtain. Outside, birds chirped like the world was still alright. Morning was too fresh. Life continued, apparently.

Leland swung his legs off the bed. The movement felt heavier than it should've. He forced himself into the shower, shaved by habit, dressed out of necessity. Each movement was mechanical. Like puppetry without a puppeteer.

Downstairs, the rituals waited: brewing coffee, setting plates, pretending. Wading through the ruins of a former life he felt disconnected from.

He brewed coffee. Set the table. Three plates. No fourth. He hadn't eaten breakfast since... well, it didn't matter. The point was, he wouldn't start today.

He covered the food on the stove. Rituals for the living, done by someone who didn't quite feel among them. His daughters depended on him. That was enough to keep going.

He sat down heavily. The feet of the chair skittered across the linoleum before setting firmly in place. A warm earthy smell filled

124

him. He took a deep breath. He stirred his coffee like it might answer something. The steam curled upward, warm and useless.

By 6:45, the table was ready— the scent of eggs and toast softening the walls. The first footfalls belonged to Angelina.

She drifted in like smoke—black-on-black clothes, black nails, blacker mood. Her lipstick drew a hard line across her mouth like it was tired of speaking for her. Her nightshirt had some cartoonish animal printed across the chest, incongruous against her armor. Her lipstick looked drawn on in ink, her eyes framed like shields.

Leland almost smiled. Then. Thought better of it.

No words came at first.

Once, she used to hover beside him, waiting for a nod before pulling out her chair next to his.

Now, she crossed the room silently, poured her coffee, and sat in the chair farthest from him.

"Morning," she muttered, not to him exactly, eyes locked on nothing.

"Morning," he said back, too softly.

She didn't hear it—or didn't want to.

Leland watched her, unsure if she was reaching out or walling off. She didn't meet his eyes.

'She used to smile.'

Now, she sat as far from him as the table allowed. Her eyes scanned the table. Three place settings. Her eyes stopped at the spot on the table in front of him.

"Hmph." But then: she moved.

She got up.

She plated food. For everyone.

Morgan's usual eggs. Catherine's toast. Even a plate for him. She didn't look up while she did it. Just filled the dishes. Her hands moved with practiced care, not affection—like checking boxes.

A glass of orange juice for Morgan, set down like a peace offering nobody asked for.

Then, out of habit or hope, she placed the third before Leland. He wouldn't touch it. He hadn't in months. But she did it anyway. Quiet. No demand. A ritual showing she hadn't abandoned everything.

She placed a glass of orange juice beside Morgan's plate—never milk. Morgan didn't like milk with breakfast anymore. That mattered. Angelina remembered.

Angelina's work was finished within minutes. She didn't look at him when she sat down again. Just folded in at the farthest edge of the small table, her presence loud in its distance.

Leland watched her. There was something almost maternal in her movements. Not warm, but exacting.

Leland looked down at the plate in front of him.

'She didn't need to care—but she did.

Somewhere beneath the armor.'

The kitchen stayed quiet until Catherine arrived, ushering Morgan in with her.

Catherine entered with a practiced smile, leading Morgan in by the wrist like a tethered balloon. Sixteen going on thirty, Catherine walked with purpose, with poise. She wore Helen's middle name and all of her calm.

"Morning, Leland," she said brightly, brushing his cheek with a kiss before sitting beside him.

Angelina's eyes snapped toward her—that name. A flash of warning mixed with anger flickered across her face. Leland. Not Dad. Not Daddy. The sharpness of it didn't go unnoticed.

Catherine caught the look, faltered for a second, but sat anyway.

"Morning, Baby Girl," he replied. It was the same exchange every morning. Like a script neither of them dared change. He nodded and smiled, small but sincere.

Morgan trailed behind, drowning in her oversized gray sweater. The sleeves swallowed her hands. Her hair curled down around her face in sleep-warmed waves.

"Morning, Daddy," she mumbled.

"Morning, Sweetie Bird. Sleep okay?" he asked.

Morgan looked up and nodded, her lips tugging into a barely-there smile. She wandered to her seat and sat, picking up her fork like it weighed something. She stirred the eggs. One push, then another. Small circles. No intent to eat.

Angelina noticed. Her gaze slid toward her sister. "You're not eating," she said, voice low, precise. Not sharp. Just... measured.

Morgan flinched. Her fork paused. Silence spread.

Not because of the tone—but because this was a pattern. Angelina noticed everything. Whether she brushed her teeth. Skipped dinner. Spoke too softly. She didn't scold. She tracked. And sometimes that stung more.

Catherine's gaze shifted toward Angelina but said nothing.

Leland noticed the tension rise.

"Let her be. She's fine," Leland said gently, not looking away from his youngest.

Angelina stiffened. Her face didn't change, but something shifted.

He'd echoed her concern—as if it were his. As if he hadn't missed all the signs she'd been tracking for weeks. She glanced down at her coffee, fingers tightening around the mug.

"No, she's not," Angelina snapped, but left it there.

"She just needs time," Leland sighed. He brushed a hand through Morgan's unruly hair.

Morgan's fork wobbled in her hand.

Morgan's eyes turned up to her father, frightened. "You'll be here when I get back... right?"

Leland's breath caught. His heart clenched. "Of course. I'll be here. I promise."

She nodded but didn't look convinced. She leaned across the space and into him briefly, wrapping small fingers around his arm. Not letting go.

He rested his hand on hers.

"Morgan," he said softly, "you have to eat, Sweetie Bird.

Angelina watched, her jaw tightened. The repeated instruction—her own concern repackaged in Leland's voice—hit her sideways. Her expression flickered. It didn't sting because of what he said—it stung because she'd said it first, and he hadn't heard her.

She looked away. Picked at her nails. Turned back to her coffee, and said nothing more.

Morgan moved the fork to her mouth. She tried a bite.

"You've got to eat more than that," Leland said quietly. "You need your strength."

One. Then another.

"Good girl," he murmured.

Morgan glanced at Angelina—guilt or apology in her eyes—then took a hesitant bite. Angelina looked down, then away. Morgan glanced at her plate again, then at Leland. "What if... you're not?"

He wanted to lie with conviction. But his voice cracked anyway. "I will be. I'll be there to pick you up, Morgan. I swear it."

Another nod. Another bite.

Small. Reluctant. But it was something.

The room fell into rhythm, if not peace.

Angelina finished first.

She stood. Cleared her plate.

She paused beside Catherine and her sister smiled hesitantly and leaned back in her chair. Angelina brushed her hair aside before leaning down and kissing her on the forehead. She moved over to Morgan, knelt beside her and gave her a lingering kiss on the cheek. She stood and ruffled her hair.

Finally, she paused behind her father. Her breath caught.

Her hand hovered—just a breath above his shoulder.

Leland noticed but continued looking at his coffee cup.

For a second, it looked like she might say something. Do something.

But the moment passed. Her fingers curled into a fist. She turned.

Gave a half-hearted wave toward the door.

She hesitated again at the threshold. Her hand brushed the wall. Breath caught in her throat.

She almost turned around.

Almost.

But didn't.

She slipped out, held together by silence. She went upstairs to get ready for school.

Leland watched her go. He caught the moment—*felt* it.

He almost reached back.

Almost.

Ten minutes later, the front door closed. A car engine started.

He stared down at the plate in front of him—still full. The bacon cooling beside untouched eggs. He tightened his grip around the coffee mug, jaw clenched behind the effort to... *'What? Say something? Do anything?'*

'For why? For what?... For who?'

Nothing came.

The silence won—*again*.

He knew it wasn't enough.

A heavy noise filled the kitchen as his shoulders slumped. He folded over the table, elbows resting uneasily on the surface.

Moments later, he shook once and glanced over at Catherine and Morgan, watching them as they finished up and cleared their plates.

Another day beginning.

He drove Catherine and Morgan to school. The day stretched ahead: people who whispered condolences under their breath, paperwork, phone calls. An endless string of obligations.

He would drink tonight.

He already knew that.

But something needed to change.

He just didn't know what or how.

Chapter 3

Janet watched as the man she had once known as vibrant and driven now moved numbly through the motions of another day. She could hardly reconcile this Leland with the confident, ambitious law student she had admired from the sidelines during their college years. Back then, she, Leland, and Helen had been inseparable—study partners, confidantes, friends. Janet had harbored a quiet crush on Leland, but she had never acted on it, knowing that his heart belonged to Helen.

Now, as she stood in the office they shared, she couldn't help but wonder what might have been if things had turned out differently. But those thoughts were fleeting, always quickly replaced by the guilt of even entertaining them. Helen had been her best friend, and Janet had loved her like a sister. Watching Leland deteriorate after Helen's death broke her heart, not just as his assistant but as someone who had cared deeply for both of them.

The law firm where they worked was one of the city's most prestigious, and Leland was a crucial partner. Janet was a junior partner and had put aside her own work to act as his aid. His expertise in corporate law had been the backbone of the firm's success for years. Colleagues often looked to him for guidance, and his clients trusted him implicitly. But that was before Helen's death. Now, whispers circulated through the firm's sleek, modern hallways.

"He hasn't been the same since..."

"His work is slipping."

"I don't think he's going to last much longer."

Janet had heard it all, and each comment made her wince. She had worked tirelessly to keep Leland afloat, managing the small details he let slip through the cracks, ensuring that his reputation remained intact. She had even shielded him from the office politics that had started to swirl as other partners eyed his position, sensing weakness.

The firm had always been a competitive environment, but lately, it had become cutthroat. Leland's absence from key meetings and his failure to bring in new clients hadn't gone unnoticed. Janet had tried to cover for him, but there was only so much she could do. The younger associates, hungry for recognition, had started circling like vultures. She had overheard one of them, a particularly ambitious junior partner named Ethan, openly speculating about how soon Leland might step down.

Still, Janet remained fiercely protective of him. She had seen the toll grief had taken on Leland, and she knew he was still the brilliant lawyer he had always been—if only he could find a way to reconnect with his work. She did everything she could to create a buffer between him and the rest of the firm. But as the days passed, she worried that her efforts might not be enough.

"Leland... Leland," Janet said gently, trying to pull him out of the fog that seemed to envelop him these days.

Leland looked up slowly, as if emerging from a deep trance. It took him a moment to register who was speaking, and then he managed a faint smile. "Janet," he said, his voice tinged with exhaustion.

"I'm heading home for the evening," she continued, her tone soft but firm. "The day is done."

Leland blinked, glancing around the office as if seeing it for the first time. He hadn't realized how late it had gotten. Papers were strewn across his desk, and the once-tidy space was cluttered with unfinished tasks. He felt a pang of guilt, knowing that Janet had likely been the one keeping everything together while he drifted.

"Thank you, Janet," he murmured, his voice barely above a whisper. "I'll see you in the morning."

Janet nodded, but she lingered for a moment longer, her eyes searching his face. "Leland, if you ever need to talk... about anything... I'm here."

He met her gaze, and for a brief second, she thought she saw a flicker of the old Leland—the man who had been so full of life, so full of plans for the future. But just as quickly, it was gone, replaced by the same distant look she had come to dread.

"Thanks," he said, and with that, Janet knew the conversation was over. She handed him his briefcase and watched as he moved like a marionette, wooden and stiff, gathering his things to leave. It would be the same routine tomorrow, she knew. And the day after that.

As she left the office, Janet couldn't shake the feeling of helplessness that had settled over her. She wished she could do more—something to snap Leland out of his grief, to bring him back to the world of the living. But she knew that was a journey he had to make on his own.

Once the office was empty, Leland sat back down, staring at the papers on his desk. He had made the phone calls, signed the documents, and attended the meetings, but he couldn't remember a single thing he had done. It was all a blur. For the first time, he felt a flicker of fear. He was losing himself, and he didn't know how to stop it.

His thoughts drifted back to Janet. She had been such a constant in his life, always there with a steady hand and a kind word. He thought about how Helen had introduced them back in college, laughing as she told Leland that Janet would keep him in line. And she had, for all these years. But now, he wondered if even Janet's unwavering support would be enough to pull him out of the darkness.

Leland finally gathered his things and left the office, the weight of the day pressing down on him like a physical burden. He picked up his daughters and went home, the same routine playing out as it had for months. But as he lay in bed that night, staring at the ceiling, he couldn't shake the feeling that something had to change.

Chapter 4

The colors blurred into a dull, oppressive haze. Leland's vision struggled to separate the hues, to make sense of the swirling chaos around him. But he failed—everything remained a muddled wash of indistinguishable tones.

His emotions churned, shifting with the light. No, that wasn't it—the light shifted with his emotions. Flashes of red-hot anger, ocean-deep sorrow, and inky black despair charged the air, stretching from horizon to horizon. The landscape around him mirrored the subtle yet volatile changes within him.

He became aware that he was kneeling, the cold ground pressing against his legs. Something—no, someone—lay in his lap. Tears streamed freely down his face, the inevitable truth already weighing on his chest. The face below him, once so alive and vibrant, now held only a lifeless stillness. Those once-bright eyes, which had burned with the fire of life, stared blankly into his own. The unasked question, Why?, clung to her lips, frozen in time.

The world around them was a suffocating black void, and he found himself painted in an ice-blue hue, stark against the darkness. In this dream—this nightmare—the woman in his arms was colored in deep, blood-tinged red. Her hands were clasped across her belly, but something seeped between those interlaced fingers. A light, fragile and fading, slipped out, escaping despite his desperate efforts to hold it in.

He pressed his hands over hers, trying to stem the flow, to keep that flickering light from slipping away. But no matter how hard he tried, it continued to seep through his fingers. Panic clawed at him as he looked around, seeking help. But all he saw were countless disembodied eyes, staring at him from the darkness. They watched him with hopelessness, unable or unwilling to offer aid. They couldn't help him. No one could.

5:45 a.m.

Leland finally stirred just before 6:00 a.m., the familiar weight of sleep clinging to him like a heavy blanket. Despite being awake for fifteen minutes, the drowsiness refused to lift. He turned his head on the pillow and came face to face with the empty space beside him. The sheets were cold, untouched, a stark reminder of how long it had been since anyone had lain there. His eyes drifted to the pillowcase, close enough to see the fine lines of thread and the thin layer of dust that had settled. Untouched. Unmoved. Irreversible.

He remained bound to the past, unable to step forward, because moving on would mean letting her go.

A sharp pang gripped his chest, and he instinctively brought his hand up to it as thoughts of Helen washed over him. The sudden rush of memory made his breath catch. He tried to push it away, but it was like trying to stop the tide. Tears welled in his eyes, and he clenched his fists, pressing them against his face in a desperate attempt to hold back the sob that threatened to break free. After a few moments, he forced himself to get out of bed, dragging his body into the morning routine, even though every step felt like wading through molasses.

As he stepped into the hallway, he nearly collided with Angelina. She stood there, wrapped in a towel, her hair still damp from the shower. Her blue eyes, the same shade as her mother's, traced over him—from the disheveled hair to the stubble on his chin. For a brief moment, there was something soft in her gaze, a flicker of concern that reminded him of the sea, deep and unfathomable. But then, like a door slamming shut, her expression hardened, her eyes turning to ice.

Without a word, Angelina squared her shoulders, her arms folding across her chest in a defensive posture. It was a gesture he knew all too well—Helen used to do the same thing when she was upset. The realization hit him like a punch to the gut. Had Angelina picked up this habit from her mother? Did she even realize it?

He watched her as she turned and walked away, her movements stiff and deliberate. She didn't look back as she disappeared down the hall, presumably heading to her room. The silence in the house seemed to grow louder with her departure, and Leland found himself staring after her, feeling more alone than ever.

The echoes of their unspoken words lingered in the air, but Leland remained frozen, unable to bridge the growing distance between them.

The day passed much like every other day since... what was her name? Helen. The thought finally surfaced, and this time, it didn't break him.

Leland was lost in his thoughts until a small voice brought him back to reality.

"Daddy?"

Morgan's voice was soft, but the concern in her eyes was unmistakable—she didn't try to hide it like her older sister did. Her gaze grounded him, pulling him back to the present, to the here and now. He looked down at the paper in front of him. He was supposed to be helping her with a simple math problem, something that shouldn't have required much effort. But he struggled to focus. His mind was elsewhere, drifting through memories and what-ifs. Morgan, patiently waiting, just wanted to know if she had done it right.

"Yes, sweetheart, that's right," Leland said, his voice gentle. He shifted in his chair, feeling the stiffness in his limbs, and decided to get up. He needed to stretch, to move, to escape the weight of the moment.

"Where ya goin', Daddy?" Morgan asked as he made his way toward the kitchen. She didn't wait for a response before the tears began to well up, spilling down her rosy cheeks.

The school counselor had called it a phase. Morgan's need to be near him, to hold on to him, had become constant. She clung to him, afraid to let go, afraid that if she did, he might vanish just like her mother had. Bedtime was the hardest—prying her fingers from his shirt or her arms from around his neck had become a nightly battle. The counselor had said she needed to feel secure, that she feared he wouldn't come back if he left her sight.

Leland knew it wasn't just about bedtime. Morgan was fine at school, as long as he promised to pick her up afterward. But that one day, when work and traffic had delayed him by fifteen minutes, she had been hysterical by the time he arrived. It had taken nearly two hours to calm her down, and the teachers were at a loss. Nothing had worked—only his presence could soothe her.

Reaching the kitchen, Leland stopped and held out his hand, waiting for Morgan to grab it. She did, her small fingers slipping into his as they walked together in silence. His thoughts drifted again, but Morgan's quiet sniffles pulled him back. He glanced down at her, watching her wipe the tears from her eyes as they moved through the house. Each step felt heavy, burdened by unspoken fears that neither of them knew how to address.

Angelina sat at the kitchen table, her voice a quiet hum as she spoke into the phone. The moment she caught her father's eyes, she quickly ended the conversation and walked out of the room without a word. Leland didn't follow her with his gaze; his focus shifted to Morgan. He found her a snack, ensuring she ate something before bedtime, and later tucked her into bed with a gentle goodnight.

Afterward, Leland found himself in the familiar comfort of a bottle of whiskey and a glass. He cradled the drink as he made his way to the bedroom, where the memories weighed the heaviest. Opening the door, he paused, noticing Catherine seated at her mother's dressing table. She was brushing her long hair, the soft strokes methodical and soothing. When she noticed him, she smiled—a warm, familiar expression that caught him off guard. Hesitantly, he returned the smile, though his heart ached at the sight of her.

Of all three girls, Catherine bore the closest resemblance to her mother. Her fine hair, golden in color, cascaded over her shoulder and into her hand as she brushed it. The way the light caught the strands made them shimmer, almost glowing like Helen's once did. It was as if the room held onto echoes of the past, playing tricks on his mind.

Angelina and Morgan had inherited his light brown hair, and both had been born with blue eyes that contrasted sharply with Catherine's honey-colored gaze—another gift from their mother. Now, as Catherine sat in his room, the similarities between mother and daughter were almost too much to bear.

Leland looked at her again, and for a moment, the lines between past and present blurred. Catherine's image seemed to fade, replaced by the haunting memory of Helen. It was as if she were still there, sitting in that exact spot. The thought sent a sharp pang through his chest, nearly bringing him to tears. The whiskey did little to dull the ache.

"My God, she's beautiful," he thought, the words catching in his throat. A lone tear escaped, sliding down his cheek as he turned away from Catherine's gaze. No matter how hard he tried, he couldn't keep the pain at bay. It was always there, lurking just beneath the surface, ready to consume him all over again.

"Goodnight, Cat," Leland said softly, using her pet name with a quiet, almost reluctant dismissal. He caught a glimpse of her as she put down the brush and stood up, preparing to leave. His eyes lingered on the nightgown she was wearing—one of her mother's. It fit her, but not quite. Catherine was just a bit smaller than Helen had been.

She had started wearing her mother's clothes a month or so after... No, he couldn't let his thoughts go there, not now.

Catherine brushed past him, whispering a hurried goodnight as she exited the room. Leland watched her go, a heavy silence filling the space she left behind. He closed the door, and after a few moments, he turned his attention to the bottle of whiskey he had brought to bed with him.

The whiskey helped. Or so he told himself. It dulled the edges of his pain, numbing it just enough for him to fall asleep. But deep down, Leland knew it was a lie. The alcohol didn't truly help. It merely masked the pain, made it tolerable for a little while, allowed him to avoid lying awake with his thoughts. That was the only reason he clung to it.

He despised the stuff. But he lived with it—the pain and the bottle.

As the night wore on, the bottle, too, was nearly empty. 'Only a corner left,' as they say. It was just as well. Leland wasn't just drinking anymore; he was drowning in it. Ten, maybe fifteen or twenty minutes ago, he had slipped past the point of merely drinking and had plunged headfirst into oblivion.

He'd fallen into his drink, feet first, with no clear way back.

He was drunk. He hadn't even bothered to undress. The thought crossed his mind that, at some point during the night, he might end up lying in a pool of his own misery. It wouldn't be the first time.

Someone was tugging at his shoes, socks, and trousers. He tried, weakly, to fend off the hands fumbling with his belt, but his feeble struggles were useless. He eventually gave in, and the shirt soon followed.

He could hear someone crying nearby. Leland tried to figure out why. It wasn't him—that's what the whiskey was for. To dull the pain, and his senses, enough that he could pass out without crying himself to sleep.

Voices drifted into his muddled consciousness, though the words seemed foreign, as if they were speaking a language he couldn't quite grasp.

"He reeks," Catherine muttered, her voice tight as she worked on getting his collar undone. She ignored his weak protests, her focus unwavering. Angelina had already managed to remove his socks, shoes, and pants. Now, she moved to help Catherine with the shirt.

"Morgan, I need that washcloth," Angelina instructed, her tone more commanding than usual. Leland had somehow managed to wedge his arm under his back, making it difficult to get the sleeve off.

He was rambling now, words slurred and incoherent.

"What's he saying, Angelina?" Catherine asked, her brow furrowed in concentration.

Angelina paused, listening closely to the disjointed mutterings. "He's not saying anything that makes sense," she replied, finally freeing his arm from the sleeve. Morgan stood nearby, clutching a steaming towel, her small hands struggling to wring out the excess water.

"I couldn't wring it out... it's too hot," Morgan squeaked, her voice tinged with worry as Angelina's sharp gaze fell on her.

"It's okay, sweetie bird," Angelina said, her tone softening as she took the towel. She turned to the bucket by the bed and squeezed out the remaining water, preparing for the inevitable. The bucket was there just in case their father couldn't hold down whatever remnants of whiskey were still churning in his stomach.

Angelina had come to say goodnight to her father, feeling an almost desperate need to reconnect with him in some way. She hadn't expected to find him in such a state—pale, slumped over, and dangerously close to suffocating in his own vomit. If she hadn't walked in at that moment, it might have been too late. Panic gripped her, but she quickly pushed it aside and enlisted Catherine and Morgan's help to take care of him.

After Angelina and Catherine helped Leland into bed, Morgan lingered at the door, her small frame caught in the doorway's shadow. She watched her sisters carefully, their movements hurried and precise as they settled their father. Hesitating, she finally stepped forward, her fingers gripping the edge of her nightshirt as she approached him.

She gently touched his arm, her small hand trembling slightly. "Daddy... are you okay?" Her voice was soft, but the weight of her question seemed to pierce through the fog in Leland's mind.

He turned his head sluggishly, his bleary eyes struggling to focus on her. "Mmm... fine, sweet... sweetie bird," he slurred, the words heavy and tangled on his tongue. His breath hit her with the sharp tang of whiskey, making her reel back instinctively.

Morgan scrunched her nose, recoiling slightly. "Daddy, you stink," she said, her voice filled with a mix of innocence and disgust.

Catherine quickly intervened, stepping forward and gently taking Morgan by the shoulders. "That's enough, sweetie bird. He's not feeling well right now," she said softly, her tone firm but comforting.

Morgan hesitated, looking back at Leland with wide, questioning eyes. Catherine gently guided her toward the door, whispering, "Big sis will take care of him." She glanced back at the chaotic scene behind her—the disheveled bed, their father barely conscious, and Angelina struggling to mask her own turmoil.

Morgan looked up at Catherine, uncertain. "Will he be okay?" she asked, her voice trembling.

Catherine nodded, though the certainty in her response felt forced. "Yes, he will. But right now, he just needs some rest." She gave Morgan a reassuring smile, though it faltered slightly as she led her out of the room.

As they reached the doorway, Morgan cast one last look at Leland, who was already drifting back into unconsciousness. "Don't leave us like Mommy," she whispered, more to herself than anyone else.

Catherine's grip tightened on Morgan's shoulder, and she whispered back, "He won't. I promise."

With that, they stepped out of the room, leaving Angelina to sit by their father's side.

Now, Leland was tucked into bed, and Catherine and Morgan had returned to their rooms. The house had fallen into an uneasy silence, but Angelina stayed. She couldn't bring herself to leave. She sat by his side, cradling his head in her lap as he slept fitfully, his breathing uneven. She watched him for hours, her thoughts tangled and heavy, until finally, his eyes fluttered open.

Leland blinked up at her, disoriented, and met her icy blue gaze. For a moment, they simply stared at each other in the dim light.

"You need to stop drinking so much before bed," Angelina finally said, her voice calm but firm. "You could have died tonight, and Catherine and Morgan need you."

Her words hung in the air, and the silence that followed felt sharp and uncomfortable. She continued to stare at him, her eyes piercing, as if she could drill the truth into him through sheer will.

Leland cleared his throat, the sound rough and strained. "And... what about you?" he asked, his voice barely above a whisper. "Do you need me?"

Angelina hesitated, the question catching her off guard. She broke eye contact, her gaze flickering to the side as she struggled to find the words. "I do... I just..." Her voice faltered, and she reached out, her hand brushing gently against his face. The warmth of her touch surprised him, and for a brief moment, a soft smile tugged at his lips.

But the moment was fleeting. Angelina's expression hardened again, her eyes clouding with emotions she couldn't fully articulate. The hatred she thought she felt warred with a deep, unresolved longing to hold her father close. In the end, she compromised by keeping her hand on his cheek, but her heart felt too conflicted to stay any longer.

"Goodnight, Father," she whispered through gritted teeth, her words tense and rushed. She stood quickly and left the room, leaving Leland alone with his thoughts. He lay there, staring at the ceiling, wondering what demons his eldest daughter was battling.

He wanted to think about it, to untangle the knot of worry in his chest, but exhaustion overtook him. His intentions to ponder the problem dissolved as sleep claimed him once more.

Chapter 5

Leland awoke in the afternoon to a strange warmth beside him. His head still throbbed with the remnants of last night's whiskey, and for a moment, he thought he was still dreaming. But as his eyes slowly adjusted to the dim light filtering through the curtains, he realized that the warmth wasn't a dream—it was Janet.

She was lying next to him, fully dressed of course, but nestled into the covers. The sight of her there, so out of place in his bed, caught him off guard. He blinked, trying to piece together how she had ended up beside him. His mind was sluggish, clouded by the hangover and the weight of his depression, but the longer he looked, the more he noticed.

Her dress had shifted slightly as she slept. The hem had ridden up just enough to expose a sliver of her thigh, pale against the dark fabric. A single bra strap had slipped off her shoulder, the soft material peeking out from beneath her dress. It wasn't overtly sexual, but it was enough to stir something in Leland that he hadn't felt in a long time—something that made him see Janet in a different light, not just as his colleague or friend.

The realization was disorienting. His mind struggled to reconcile the Janet he knew—the one who kept him afloat at work, who had been by his side through the worst of it—with this new, unfamiliar version of her. The woman lying beside him wasn't the steady, reliable presence he had always counted on. She was something else, something that made his heart skip a beat, and it unsettled him.

He tried to look away, to refocus on the ever-present ache in his chest, the grief that had driven him for so long. But his eyes betrayed him, drawn back to the soft curve of her shoulder, the way her hair fanned out on the pillow. It was such a simple thing, and yet it felt like a betrayal. How could he let himself be distracted by this when everything else still hurt so much?

As if sensing his gaze, Janet stirred beside him. Her eyes fluttered open, and for a moment, she looked as disoriented as he felt. But then she saw him watching her, and something shifted in the air between them.

Janet's breath hitched slightly, her gaze meeting his with a mixture of surprise and something else—something that made her feel out of place, as if she were crossing a line she shouldn't. She could feel his eyes on her, the way they lingered just a moment too long on the bare skin of her shoulder, and it sent a small thrill through her, despite the awkwardness of the situation.

She shifted, trying to adjust her dress, but the movement only made the fabric slide further, exposing more of her thigh. A flush crept up her neck, and she quickly looked away, biting her lip as she tried to make sense of what was happening. This wasn't how things were supposed to be—she was here to help him, to be the steady presence he needed, not to feel this strange thrill at the way he was looking at her.

"I'm sorry," Janet murmured, her voice barely above a whisper. "I must have fallen asleep..."

Leland cleared his throat, the sound rough in the quiet room. "No, it's... it's fine," he said, though the words felt awkward in his mouth. His eyes flicked to the ceiling, then back to her, unsure of where to settle. The energy between them was thick, charged with something neither of them knew how to address.

Janet shifted again, pulling the hem of her dress down as she sat up. She avoided his gaze, her fingers fidgeting with the fabric as she tried to regain her composure. "I just... I wanted to make sure you were okay," she added, her tone forced casual. "I didn't mean to... intrude."

Leland shook his head, trying to find the right words. "You didn't," he said, though it felt like a lie. The room suddenly felt too small, the bed too intimate, and he wasn't sure what to do with his hands, his thoughts, or the strange tension between them.

Janet finally met his gaze, her eyes searching his face for some kind of reassurance, something to ground her in this awkward moment. She could see the conflict in his eyes, the way he struggled to reconcile what was happening with everything else. And in that moment, she felt a pang of guilt, a small voice in the back of her mind telling her that she was wrong for feeling what she was feeling, for wanting something more when he was still so lost.

But that voice was quiet, drowned out by the warmth of his gaze, the way his eyes softened as they looked at her. She knew she should leave, to give him space, but instead, she lingered, the silence between them stretching out until it felt like something had shifted, something neither of them could take back.

"I should go," Janet finally said, breaking the silence. But even as she said it, she didn't move, her eyes still locked on his, waiting for him to say something, to do something that would either break the tension or make it real.

"Yeah," Leland replied, though his voice was hesitant. He knew she should go, that it would be the right thing for both of them, but a part of him didn't want her to leave. Not yet. Not when things felt so uncertain, and her presence, however awkward, was still a comfort.

But then Janet slowly rose from the bed, smoothing down her dress, and the moment passed. The tension ebbed away, leaving only the awkwardness in its wake. She gave him a small, strained smile and turned to leave, her footsteps soft as she made her way to the door.

As she reached the doorway, she hesitated, looking back at him one last time. "If you need anything, I'm here," she said, her voice quiet but sincere.

Leland nodded, his gaze lingering on her for a moment longer before she finally slipped out of the room, leaving him alone with his thoughts once more. The bed felt emptier without her, and as he stared at the ceiling, he couldn't shake the feeling that something had changed—something that neither of them were quite ready to face.

Later, Leland sat in the living room, sinking into the worn-out cushions of the couch as he tried to steady himself. The world still felt off-kilter, tilting precariously whenever he moved too quickly. He watched as Janet moved through the house with an ease that he envied. She seemed to know just where to step, just what to say, to keep the girls calm and—dare he say it—happy.

Morgan was the first to latch onto Janet, practically glued to her side as they moved from room to room. She giggled at something Janet said, her face lighting up in a way Leland hadn't seen in a long time. The sound of her laughter brought a small smile to his lips, but it quickly faded as the familiar weight of guilt crept back in. He should be the one making her laugh, not someone else.

Angelina, too, seemed to find comfort in Janet's presence. Though she was usually guarded, distant, Leland noticed how she would occasionally drift closer to Janet, standing just a little nearer, listening a little more intently. It wasn't much, but it was something. A small crack in the armor she had built around herself.

As they passed by the living room, Leland caught Janet stealing a glance at him. Their eyes met for a brief moment before she quickly looked away, focusing on Morgan, who was tugging at her sleeve, eager to show her something. Leland couldn't help but notice the way her presence seemed to fill the space, making the house feel less empty. He found himself watching her more than he wanted to admit, trying to figure out what it was that made him feel... different. But he dismissed it, chalking it up to the fact that he hadn't been close to a woman—any woman—in what felt like forever.

Dinner that night was a quiet affair, but there was a different energy at the table. The usual heaviness that hung in the air was lighter, lifted by Janet's presence and the girls' improved moods. Catherine sat beside Janet, helping her serve the food. Leland noticed how Catherine seemed more animated, more herself, as she chatted with Janet about school, her friends, and what she had been up to lately.

"Janet, can you believe that Ms. Carter actually gave us extra homework over the weekend?" Catherine said with mock outrage as she passed a dish of roasted vegetables. "I mean, seriously, who does that?"

Janet chuckled, shaking her head. "Oh, I remember those days. I had a teacher like that once. We used to call him 'Mr. Extra' because he always gave us more work than we could handle. But you know what? I bet you'll feel amazing once you finish it."

Catherine rolled her eyes playfully. "Yeah, sure. I'll be sure to thank her when I'm drowning in algebra."

Morgan giggled, her fork pausing mid-air as she joined in. "Ms. Carter sounds mean! I'm glad I don't have her yet."

Angelina, who had been quiet for most of the meal, chimed in unexpectedly. "She's not that bad, actually. Just... strict. But you can get away with a lot if you know how to play by her rules." Her tone was lighter, less guarded than usual.

Leland looked over at Angelina, surprised by her contribution. He hadn't heard her speak like that in months—so casually, without the usual sharpness in her voice. Janet had that effect, it seemed.

Janet smiled at Angelina, acknowledging her comment. "I bet you've figured out all the tricks by now, huh? You've always been clever like that."

Angelina shrugged but didn't deny it. There was a hint of a smile tugging at the corners of her mouth as she focused on her plate.

Leland watched the interaction, noting the way Janet navigated the conversation with ease, making each of his daughters feel seen, heard. She caught his eye again, and this time, she didn't look away immediately. There was something in her gaze—an unspoken understanding that made his chest tighten. He looked down at his plate, trying to shake the feeling.

"So, Leland," Catherine said, drawing his attention. "Janet's been telling us about this awesome recipe she knows. We were thinking maybe we could try it out next weekend. What do you think?"

Leland forced a smile, trying to focus on the conversation. "Yeah, sure. That sounds good. Whatever you girls want."

Catherine grinned, pleased with his response. "Great! We'll need to make a shopping list then."

As they continued to eat, Leland found himself glancing at Janet more often than he intended. She was different from anyone else who had been in his life since Helen. She wasn't trying to replace her—he knew that much—but there was a warmth in her presence, a quiet strength that he hadn't realized he missed until now. Yet every time he caught himself looking at her, he pushed the thoughts aside, reminding himself that this wasn't the time, that his emotions were too tangled to make sense of anything.

Janet, too, felt the weight of his gaze. She tried to focus on the girls, on the conversation, but she couldn't help the way her heart fluttered whenever she caught him looking at her. It was strange, this feeling—this awareness of him as something more than just her friend, her colleague. It thrilled her, but it also made her feel out of place, as if she were stepping into territory she wasn't sure she belonged in.

As they were clearing the table, Catherine reached for the last dish, but Angelina grabbed it first, her movements quick and deliberate. Catherine's smile faltered as she narrowed her eyes at her sister. "I was going to get that, Angelina," she said, her voice sharp with irritation.

Angelina shrugged, barely glancing at her. "You're always trying to do everything, Cat. Let someone else help for once. You're not mom."

Catherine's hands tightened around the dish she was holding, her frustration simmering just below the surface. "I'm just trying to keep things running smoothly. It's not a competition."

"Could've fooled me," Angelina muttered under her breath, though loud enough for Catherine to hear.

The tension crackled between them for a moment before Janet stepped in, placing a gentle hand on Catherine's shoulder. "Why don't you both take a break? I've got the rest of this," Janet said softly, her calm tone diffusing the tension as Catherine let out a small huff and reluctantly stepped back.

When dinner was over, and the dishes were cleared, Leland retreated to the living room again, grateful for the chance to sit and clear his head. The room was quiet now, the girls having gone off to do their own things. But the memory of Janet's presence lingered, and he couldn't shake the feeling that something had shifted between them.

As the evening wore on, Leland found himself staring out the window, lost in thought. He knew he had to figure out what he was feeling, to make sense of the strange tension that had settled between them. But for now, he pushed it aside, focusing instead on the small comfort of having his daughters in a better mood, of hearing their laughter again—even if it wasn't because of him.

And as he sat there, the shadows lengthening around him, he wondered what the future held, and whether he was ready to face it.

Chapter 6

Leland sat at his desk, staring blankly at the pile of files in front of him. His office, usually a place of order and precision, felt like a chaotic mess today. Papers were scattered, sticky notes clung to his monitor, and his calendar flashed with reminders that felt like distant echoes. He rubbed his temples, trying to shake off the remnants of the night before. His head still throbbed, not just from the hangover but from the weight of everything else—the grief, the guilt, the uncertainty.

Across the room, Janet was organizing her own desk, her movements deliberate and efficient. She had always been like that, Leland thought—steady, dependable. But now, every time he looked at her, he couldn't help but see something different. The memory of her lying beside him, her dress slightly askew, lingered in his mind. It wasn't just the physicality of it that unsettled him, but the way it had made him feel.

She wasn't just his colleague anymore, or even just his friend. She was a woman—a woman who had stirred something in him that he hadn't felt in years. And that realization terrified him.

He tried to push the thoughts away, to focus on the work in front of him, but it was like trying to hold back a tidal wave. The more he tried to ignore it, the stronger it became. And then, like a dam breaking, the thoughts came rushing in. What was he doing? Why was he letting himself get distracted by this when there were so many more important things at stake?

"Leland, do you need me to go over the details of the Parker case with you again before the meeting?" Janet's voice broke through his thoughts, pulling him back to the present.

He looked up at her, and for a moment, the words caught in his throat. She was standing there, file in hand, her usual professional demeanor firmly in place. But now, all he could see was the memory of her lying beside him, her dress riding up just enough to expose a sliver of skin. He blinked, forcing the image away, trying to refocus on the matter at hand.

"Uh, no... I think I've got it," he said, though his voice lacked conviction.

Janet hesitated, sensing his distraction. She had been feeling off-balance all morning, ever since she had woken up in his bed. Fully clothed, sure, but it had still felt... intimate. Too intimate. She had overstepped her bounds, she knew that. And now, standing here, she couldn't shake the feeling of guilt that clung to her like a shadow.

"Are you sure? Because if you're not ready—"

"I'm fine, Janet. Really," Leland interrupted, though he could see the doubt in her eyes. He quickly added, "And... about last night. It was... it was okay. You used to come over all the time before. The girls... they smiled again. All of them. That was because of you."

Janet's heart skipped a beat at his words, but she quickly tamped down the feelings that rose in response. This wasn't the time. She needed to focus, to be the professional that Leland needed her to be right now. Still, she couldn't ignore the warmth that spread through her at his acknowledgment. The crush she'd had on him back in college had never truly gone away—it had just been buried under years of professionalism and respect. But now, those feelings were surfacing with a force she couldn't deny.

"Leland, about last night... I just wanted to say that I'm sorry if I overstepped. I didn't mean to make things awkward."

Leland shook his head, a small smile tugging at the corners of his mouth. "You didn't overstep, Janet. If anything, I should be thanking you. You made a difference—for me and for the girls."

Janet nodded, her guilt easing slightly, but not entirely. She had put off her own responsibilities to help Leland, and now she was wondering if it had been worth it. Not because she didn't want to help him—of course she did—but because it was starting to blur the lines between what she was supposed to be doing and what she wanted to do. And that scared her.

Thinking time was his ally, Leland stepped out of his office, heading toward the restroom. This routine had become his ritual—a quiet moment to gather his thoughts, to prepare himself for whatever meeting or challenge awaited him. In the solitude of the restroom, he stood before the mirror, muttering softly to himself. It was a habit that his colleagues had grown accustomed to over the years. Associates and paralegals came and went, barely acknowledging him as they passed by, knowing this was just Leland's way of getting into the zone.

A new paralegal, however, wasn't as familiar with Leland's routine. He entered the restroom with a more seasoned colleague and paused, watching Leland with curiosity. "What's he doing?" he whispered.

His companion, a paralegal who had been with the firm for some time, quickly guided him out of the restroom. "That's just his thing before meetings," he explained, shaking his head with a small smile. "Don't worry about it. It's fine."

Leland, lost in his own world, remained undistracted by their presence. For the first time in what felt like ages, he felt a sense of clarity, a focus that had eluded him for so long. The brief exchange between the paralegals didn't register—his thoughts were finally where they needed to be, centered on the task at hand.

Meanwhile, Janet remained in the office, seated at her desk, juggling papers and emails in an effort to keep Leland focused on the important tasks ahead. She was the anchor, the one who had to make sure everything stayed on track, especially with the big meeting looming. Just as she was about to hit send on a response, the door to Leland's office swung open, and Ethan strode in with his usual grating arrogance.

"Hey, is Leland ready for the big meeting with Parker? Oh, wait," he paused dramatically, glancing at the clock on the wall, "looks like he missed it."

Janet's stomach clenched. "What do you mean, missed it?"

Ethan smirked, clearly relishing the moment. "The meeting started an hour ago. He didn't show, so my boss had to step in and handle things. You're welcome, by the way."

Janet's face went pale. How could they have both missed it? Guilt surged through her. She was supposed to keep Leland on track, to make sure he didn't miss anything crucial. Frantically, she checked the firm's intranet calendar. Her worst fears were confirmed—the meeting had been rescheduled. She had been operating under the assumption it was still set for the following day, and now everything was falling apart.

Ethan's smug grin widened as he watched the realization hit her. "You sure aren't doing your job well."

"That's enough, Ethan," Janet snapped, her voice sharp. "You might want to check your facts before you start gloating. The briefing notes said the meeting was scheduled for tomorrow morning. So why weren't we informed ahead of time? Now, Leland has missed an important meeting, and we could lose this client because of it. You could have mentioned something when you noticed it was off—you're just as responsible for this mess."

Ethan sneered. "You're his secretary. That's your job. But thanks for your concern."

Janet's eyes narrowed as she stood up from her desk, her posture rigid. "I'm not a secretary, Ethan. I'm acting as his assistant, yes, but I'm also a partner in this firm. You're still just a junior partner. You'd do well to remember that."

Ethan's smug expression faltered, and he stammered, searching for a retort, but Janet didn't give him the chance.

"I think I'll have a word with the partner you're working under," Janet continued, her tone icy. "Maybe it's time to reassess whether you're still needed here."

Ethan's bravado crumbled. "I—uh—I'll double-check why you weren't notified," he mumbled, his confidence shattered as he quickly retreated from the office.

As the door closed behind him, Janet sank back into her chair, the tension lingering in the air. She couldn't shake the guilt gnawing at her. How could she have let this happen? How had she let everything slip? And worse, why did she feel so conflicted about last night, when she should have been focused on work?

She took a deep breath, trying to steady herself. But Leland's absence from the meeting was just one more reminder that things were unraveling faster than she could manage.

Janet hurried down the hall to find Andrew, Ethan's supervisor, and the one who had stepped in for Leland during the Parker meeting. When she returned to Leland's office, she found him seated at his desk, his expression distant.

Hesitating at the door, Janet folded her hands in front of her, staring at her feet as she tried to find the right words. "Um, Leland... I... You missed the meeting," she stammered, her voice barely above a whisper.

Leland's stomach dropped. "What do you mean, missed it?"

"The meeting started an hour ago," Janet explained. "It's already over."

Leland's shoulders slumped as the weight of her words hit him. His face drained of color as he realized the importance of what he had missed. His responsibilities, the work he prided himself on—he had let it all slip. Worry clouded his eyes as he stared off into the distance, his thoughts spinning in a haze of regret and uncertainty. "What do I do now..."

Janet's own guilt surged, a wave crashing over her as she struggled to process how they had both let this happen. She had been there to keep him on track, to make sure he didn't miss anything crucial, and yet, here they were. But fortunately, she had reached out to Andrew, who had assured her that everything was fine, though he hadn't provided many details. Just as she opened her mouth to apologize, Andrew stepped into the office.

"Hey, Leland," Andrew greeted, his tone friendly and relaxed, a stark contrast to the tension in the room. Despite Ethan's earlier insinuations, Andrew didn't seem interested in replacing Leland. Closing the door behind him, he offered Janet a reassuring touch on the shoulder. "It's alright," he said softly before stepping past her and sitting in the chair in front of Leland's desk.

"Leland, I went ahead and filled in for you. I just wanted to let you know, I'm not trying to steal your client or anything," Andrew said, his tone more comforting than accusatory.

"What happened, Andrew?" Leland asked, his voice heavy with resignation.

Andrew sighed, glancing briefly at Janet before returning his focus to Leland. They had known each other for years, and the history between them weighed on the moment. "Look, Leland," he began, his voice gentle, "I've noticed how you've been lately, and I was worried. The senior partners rescheduled the meeting last night after you left to pick up your daughters. I didn't want you stressing any more than you already have been. You've been through a lot, and I didn't want this to make things worse for you."

He leaned forward, placing a file on the desk. "Here are the notes from the meeting. You didn't miss anything that can't be fixed."

Andrew stood to leave, but before he did, he turned back to Leland. "I'm here for you too, man. Whatever you need, just let me know." He placed a hand on Janet's shoulder again as he passed by her. "I don't want you to fail either, Janet. We're all in this together."

Leland felt a wave of relief wash over him. He hadn't completely failed; there were others looking out for him, just as he had always looked out for others. He managed a weak smile as Andrew left the office, closing the door quietly behind him.

Janet remained, watching as tears began to slip down Leland's cheeks. A mixture of relief and longing stirred within her. On one hand, she was grateful that others were stepping in to help Leland, but on the other, she found herself wanting to wrap her arms around him, to comfort him in a way that went beyond their professional relationship. But in the end, she stayed rooted in place, torn between her desire to help and her uncertainty about crossing that line. She eventually felt the need to step out of the office for a moment.

As the door clicked shut behind Andrew, Leland let out a long breath, leaning back in his chair. The relief of not having completely failed barely dulled the sharp sting of guilt that gnawed at him. His eyes fell to the pile of files on his desk, but they seemed like distant objects in a fog, barely visible through the haze of his thoughts.

He pressed his palms to his eyes, trying to block out the noise in his head. How had he let it come to this? He used to be so meticulous, so on top of everything. Every detail, every case, every client—it all used to be second nature to him. Now, it was like trying to grasp water, everything slipping through his fingers.

His mind wandered back to a time when he had been at the top of his game. He could see it so clearly—standing in the conference room, presenting a case with confidence, knowing he had everything under control. The admiration in his colleagues' eyes, the satisfaction of a job well done—it was all a far cry from where he was now. That Leland seemed like a ghost, haunting the edges of his memory, reminding him of what he had lost.

A wave of grief surged through him, and he had to choke back the sob that threatened to escape. It wasn't just his work that he had let slip; it was everything. His daughters, his home, his life—it all felt like it was crumbling around him, and he didn't know how to stop it.

He lowered his hands, staring at the files again, but this time, his focus sharpened. He couldn't let this continue. He had to find a way back, to regain control. But the question that lingered, haunting him, was how? How could he find his way back when everything felt so hopelessly lost?

Janet stood in the hallway outside Leland's office, her hand resting on the doorframe. She could hear the faint sound of his breathing, heavy and uneven, and it tugged at something deep inside her. She had always cared for Leland, had always admired his strength and dedication. But this—this was different. The feelings that had once been a mere crush in college were now something far more powerful, more undeniable.

She had never intended for this to happen. She had been so careful, so professional all these years. But seeing him like this, so broken and vulnerable, had stirred something in her that she couldn't ignore. She found herself wanting to be more than just his colleague, more than just the person who kept him on track. She wanted to be there for him in a way that went beyond the office, to be the one who could help him heal.

But that scared her. She wasn't sure if she could handle it, or if he even wanted that from her. What if she was misreading everything? What if she was only complicating things further?

She leaned her head against the doorframe, closing her eyes for a moment. She had to be careful. This wasn't just about her feelings; it was about what was best for Leland. And right now, what he needed most was stability, not more confusion.

With a deep breath, she straightened up and pushed the door open, stepping back into the office. She would be there for him, just as she always had been. But she had to keep her emotions in check, no matter how difficult it was becoming.

As Janet reentered the office, Leland's gaze drifted to her. He watched as she moved with quiet efficiency, gathering papers and organizing the desk that had become a mess of documents. There was something different in the way he saw her now, something that made his heart beat just a little faster.

He had always known Janet was dependable, but now he noticed things he hadn't before. The way her hair caught the light when she moved, the softness in her expression when she wasn't concentrating so hard. And then there was the way she had looked at him last night, the warmth in her eyes when she had held his gaze just a second too long. It had stayed with him, lingering in the back of his mind, refusing to be dismissed.

He tried to shake it off, to focus on the work in front of him, but his thoughts kept wandering back to her. She had always been there for him, yes, but now it felt different. He couldn't quite put his finger on it, but it was as if the boundary between them had shifted, the professional distance blurring into something more personal.

"Leland, are you okay?" Janet's voice broke through his thoughts, and he looked up to find her watching him, concern etched into her features.

He forced a smile, nodding. "Yeah, I'm fine. Just... thinking."

She gave him a small, understanding smile, but there was a hint of something else in her eyes—something that mirrored what he was feeling. He didn't know what to do with it, didn't know how to process the fact that, for the first time in a long time, he was noticing a woman again. Not just any woman—Janet.

The thought unsettled him, and he quickly looked away, pretending to focus on the papers in front of him. He couldn't afford to get distracted, not now. But as she moved around the office, he found his eyes drawn back to her, wondering if she had noticed the shift between them, too.

As Leland sat there, his thoughts spiraled into deeper territory. Was *this*—this new burgeoning feeling for Janet—a betrayal of the love he had for Helen? The thought gnawed at him, tugging at the raw edges of his grief. Helen had been his everything, the love of his life.

How could he possibly entertain the idea of feeling something for someone else? But then, the reality hit him like a cold wave—Helen was gone. She wasn't coming back, no matter how tightly he clung to her memory. And that was the crux of it, wasn't it?

He couldn't figure out if noticing Janet in this new light was a betrayal or just a painful acknowledgment of the fact that his life was moving forward, whether he wanted it to or not. The confusion sat heavy in his chest, a mix of guilt and uncertainty that left him questioning everything he thought he knew about love, loss, and the future that awaited him.

Chapter 7

Leland could still recall that evening as if it had happened only yesterday. The night had been a surprise for Helen—something spontaneous and completely unexpected. They had shared an early dinner, and then afterward, he had taken her to the theater. The play had enchanted her, leaving her with that radiant smile he cherished so much. That smile was what he remembered most clearly.

Once, the world had been vibrant and full of color—bright, warm, and cheerful. But now, everything was draped in a dark, rich, blood-red monochrome that obscured his vision. The brightness had vanished, replaced by a cold, hateful emptiness that seeped into every corner of his soul.

He heard voices raised in anger, distant yet unnervingly close. As he turned to locate the source of the commotion, he saw them—two men, their confrontation escalating. The distance between them seemed like a chasm, but in reality, they were far closer than he could have ever imagined. A sound, like distant thunder, erupted from their direction, followed by a flash of light that streaked through the space separating him from the chaos.

Too late, Leland realized where that beam of light was headed. Too late to pull Helen out of harm's way. Too late to shield her with his own body. The screams that followed echoed in his mind, piercing the night—or was it night? Yes, it had to be.

He found himself kneeling on the cold ground, cradling Helen's head in his lap. His hands were pressed against her stomach, desperate to stop the flow of light that seeped through his fingers like hot liquid, dripping onto the unforgiving pavement.

Her eyes, once so full of life, were now dull, searching his own with an expression that would haunt him forever. The look in her eyes, the unspoken question on her lips... it was too much to bear.

Leland rolled out of bed, his shirt clinging to his back, soaked with sweat. He knew the reason why and didn't bother questioning it. At least this time, he hadn't cried out during the night. The days of waking up in tears had passed, replaced by the dull, persistent ache of acceptance. The fire within him that once raged had dwindled to embers, threatening to extinguish entirely if he couldn't find the strength to fight it. But that strength felt elusive, slipping further away with each passing day.

He moved through his morning routine with a detached numbness—shower, dress, and then to the kitchen to find something for breakfast. By 7:30, he was seated in the living room, reading the paper while sipping his coffee. The house was still quiet; his girls were out of school for the summer, and they had taken to sleeping in. Except for Catherine. She had always been an early riser, and sure enough, it was she who wandered into the living room to greet him.

"Good morning, Leland," she said cheerfully, her voice breaking the silence.

Leland looked up from his paper, and the sight of her caught him off guard. In that instant, two things hit him: first, that his little girl had grown up without him really noticing, and second, how much she had changed in the last few months. The morning light framed her figure, revealing the subtle curves that hadn't been there before. Her hips had filled out, giving her a new softness that replaced the thinness of her younger years. Her bust had grown, too—she no longer had the boyish figure she'd once had.

But it wasn't just her figure that had changed. The tomboy he remembered had been replaced by someone who wore makeup, dresses, and... whatever she was wearing now.

Leland's gaze sharpened as he took in the sight before him, leading to the second jarring realization of the morning—Catherine was no longer wearing her own clothes. She had started wearing her mother's things, including the chemise she had on now. The delicate fabric draped down her hips, stopping abruptly, and the most disconcerting part was that it was sheer.

The sight of her surprised him. Two things struck him at once: first, that his little girl had grown up—and second, how much she resembled her mother.

She was wearing Helen's chemise. He recognized it instantly. The way it draped, the way the fabric caught the light—it was identical to the way Helen used to wear it.

Something twisted in his gut. For a split second, his body reacted before his mind caught up.

God, he thought, horror blooming like fire in his chest. What the hell is wrong with me?

It wasn't arousal. It wasn't anything like that. It was grief, memory, biology colliding in a terrible moment of confusion.

And just as quickly, it passed—replaced by shame, anger, and a blinding need to make it stop.

Catherine moved around the couch, the only barrier between them, and approached her father. She leaned down and kissed him on the cheek, a gesture that would have been innocent enough had she been wearing anything else.

For the first time in what felt like ages, Leland felt a surge of real emotion—something other than the persistent sadness that had weighed him down. Anger flashed in his eyes, hot and sudden. Catherine saw it and instinctively took a step back, recognizing the dangerous glint in her father's gaze.

"What are you wearing?" Leland hissed, his voice tight with barely restrained fury.

Catherine stammered, searching for an explanation that wouldn't make things worse. She had only seen her father this angry only twice in her life, and it had always been terrifying. The last time she had witnessed it was when he and her mother had a heated argument years ago, and once more when someone had broken into their house while the family was away.

She was still fumbling for the right words when Leland suddenly stood up, grabbed her roughly by the arm, and spun her around. The air seemed to whistle as his hand sliced through it, landing a hard swat on her behind. The force of it made her jump, the sting of the blow leaving her shocked and speechless.

Catherine crumpled to the floor, her body trembling with shock. Tears streamed down her face as she alternated between rubbing the sting on her bottom and wiping her eyes. The impact of what had just happened left her reeling, and she sobbed uncontrollably.

The sound of her scream, echoing in the room, snapped Leland out of his furious haze. Guilt and disbelief washed over him as he realized what he had done. He bent down quickly, scooping Catherine up into his arms, his heart aching with regret. He had never laid a hand on any of his daughters before. The shock of his own actions mirrored the shock in Catherine's tear-filled eyes.

"Cat," he began, his voice thick with remorse, "I'm so sorry. I didn't mean to do that." He held her close as she continued to cry, her face buried in his chest, her arms wrapped tightly around his neck. They stayed like that for what felt like an eternity, her sobs gradually subsiding into quiet sniffles. Leland cradled her in his strong arms, offering the only comfort he could. He could feel how small and fragile she was, just like Helen had been—barely more than ninety pounds.

As Catherine's tears finally slowed, Leland pressed a gentle kiss to her forehead. "I don't mind you wearing your mother's clothes, Cat, but this...," he hesitated, realizing he needed to explain why he had reacted so strongly. She was old enough now, and she deserved to understand.

"I got so angry when I saw you wearing this," he admitted, his voice soft but firm.

Catherine sniffled, looking up at him with red, puffy eyes. "Why?" she asked, her voice barely above a whisper.

Leland sighed, gathering his thoughts. "You shouldn't wear anything like this in front of any man that you aren't in a relationship with—an intimate relationship. It's just... It's not appropriate, Cat."

He kissed her forehead again, his touch gentle as he slowly set her down on her feet. "Go get changed, Cat," he suggested softly. "You and Morgan are spending the day with me."

Catherine nodded silently, still processing everything that had happened. She turned and made her way upstairs, the weight of the morning lingering between them both. Leland watched her go, his heart heavy with the realization of how fragile their relationship had become—and how much he needed to protect it.

Leland sat down heavily, a deep sigh escaping him. The air whistled through his teeth as he muttered, "Goddammit," to no one in particular. He was exhausted—mentally and emotionally drained. The weight of what had just happened bore down on him, leaving him horrified by the fact that he had lost control and struck his own child. He had always known his strength, always feared that in anger, he could unintentionally hurt his daughters. He had promised himself long ago that he would never raise a hand to discipline them. Until now, he had never needed to, and he had thanked God for that. The girls had always seemed naturally inclined to do the right thing. But everything had changed, and so had they.

In the span of a few months, their once stable lives had spiraled into uncertainty. Leland felt the crushing weight of responsibility for all of it. He blamed himself for the turmoil that had invaded their lives, for the pain and confusion that seemed to follow them at every turn. Catherine's choice of dress wasn't his fault. Morgan's fear of losing another parent wasn't his fault. Angelina's anger at what she perceived as his failure to be there for them wasn't his fault either. Yet, he couldn't shake the overwhelming guilt. All their hurts, pains, and frustrations felt like a three-course meal set before him, ready to be consumed. He swallowed it all, believing he had no choice, feeling trapped in the vice of depression that seemed to choke the life out of him.

Catherine and Morgan came downstairs sometime later, finding him staring blankly out the window, lost in thought. His mind raced, the guilt and despair looping endlessly, but he forced himself to pull it together for their sake. He managed a weak smile and took the two girls out to lunch, hoping to create some semblance of normalcy. Angelina had declined to join them, preferring to spend the day with Janet, who had become a closer confidant over the past few months.

After lunch, they visited a small local amusement park, though Leland's heart wasn't in it. He went through the motions, his body present but his mind far away, barely registering the minor moments happening around him. The laughter of his daughters, the bright colors of the park, the feel of the sun on his face—it all felt distant, muted by the fog of his own thoughts. He couldn't shake the feeling that he was failing them, even as he tried to be there for them.

Leland handed the girls money to buy whatever they wanted and stood with them in line for rides, trying his best to play the part of an attentive father. Yet, for most of the day, the girls felt as if they were with a complete stranger. He avoided any physical contact with Catherine, a palpable tension hanging between them. Morgan, sensing the distance, found herself standing between them on more than one occasion, as if trying to bridge the gap that had formed. Eventually, Catherine gave up seeking his approval or attention, retreating into herself, the morning's incident still fresh in her mind. She felt lost, confused, and unsure of where she stood with her father now.

They left the amusement park late that evening, stopping to grab a quick bite to eat. The girls assumed the day was winding down, but Leland had one more surprise for them—a movie. Unfortunately, it didn't go as smoothly as he had hoped.

After settling the girls into their seats, Leland excused himself to go to the restroom and grab some snacks. The lines were longer than expected, and by the time he was heading back to the theater, he heard the unmistakable sound of screaming.

"I want my daddy! Cat, is daddy coming back?"

Rushing down the corridor, Leland's heart sank when he saw his daughters in the hallway. Morgan was in tears, her voice trembling with fear, while an usher stood helplessly beside them, trying in vain to calm her. The woman looked nearly as distressed as Morgan, clearly struggling with the situation. Catherine knelt beside her sister, holding her in a protective hug, her face a mix of worry and relief as she spotted their father hurrying toward them.

Leland immediately dropped the snacks into the nearest trash can and sprinted to them, his heart pounding. His words of thanks to the usher and reassurances to Morgan echoed down the hallway as he gathered his daughters and led them out of the theater. The movie was forgotten, as was the rest of the evening. Later, when Leland tried to recall the film they were supposed to see, the title slipped from his memory—just another detail lost in the haze of the day.

He sprawled out on the couch.

"Who the hell am I fooling. I can't even get my own shit together, let alone help these girls."

He shifted. Precariously perched on the edge of the couch. His head found solace in the palm of his conjoined hands.

"Self-deception. Yeah, that's an option. Something easier than dealing with the minutiae of the day and the pain that comes with it."

Leland felt he'd rather be dragged naked across the sands of a desert than deal with his grief.

He hoped this night would give him some measure of relief.

Chapter 8

He walked into the kitchen.

She was there.

Helen.

Sitting like she belonged in the moment. Comfortable. As if there was more time left in this minute than there had been when a minute had first been envisioned. There were no extra seconds, but you couldn't tell her that.

She had a coffee cup in her hands. Her jeans fit just right—like they'd been measured, cut, and sewn for her alone, though he knew she bought them off the rack. Her top? A plain t-shirt. No patterns. No symbols. Just fabric. It reminded him of how she used to talk about makeup—"Unnecessary. Decoration, not definition."

Her hair was pulled back into a simple bun. Her face wasn't cold, but it wasn't open either. Not stone. Just... still. Like someone who wasn't refusing company, but also wasn't inviting it.

Most days, she would've been in something more comfortable. One of his shirts. Nothing underneath but modesty. But not tonight.

There was a line at her chin. A faint one. Like a crack you didn't know was there until light hit it just right. He squinted.

How long has that been there? He blinked. Shook his head. It was gone when he looked again.

He must have been staring, because now he was sitting beside her at the counter. He didn't remember walking the space. Just... blink, and there he was.

She was closer now. At least physically. Gazing in what should have been her flawless face, Leland found the edges fuzzy. Helen didn't look like Helen anymore. Who this was, he wasn't quite sure. Her features refused to come into clear focus.

He glanced away and then back—still hazy. Still not *her*. His gut told him to believe it was Helen. His mind disagreed. That face was a memory misremembered.

She glanced at him. Not questioning. Just recognition. A moment's awareness. He looked worn to her. He knew that look—grief had settled into his face and refused to move out. Set up shop behind his eyes. An unwelcome tenant.

"You told me..." he started.

The words hit a wall. Died there.

Her hand on his cheek stopped him.

She leaned in and kissed him on the cheek. Or tried to. He shifted. Just enough. The kiss missed. Landed... somewhere. But not where it was supposed to.

She didn't act wounded. Just stood. Stretched. Walked to the door like the warmth in the room walked with her.

At the threshold, she looked back. Once.

Her lips moved. Words he couldn't hear. He saw them. Felt them.

The fridge's compressor kicked on. Microwave beeped. The static from the TV, some late-night snow drifting across the screen. White noise.

He didn't need to hear. He knew.

I'll be back soon.

It was always that lie.

The one wrapped in ritual. The one she'd told with a smile that always bent upward, just enough to pretend she believed it. Even when neither of them did.

The door closed behind her.

Now... this was now.

The air shifted. Stagnant. Unkind. He didn't move.

A dusty cup sat on the counter where she'd been. He looked down at it. Empty. Dry. A thin coat of debris in the bottom. Neglect collected like time.

He hadn't wanted to put it away.

His hands rose to his face. Shoulders shook.

"You told me you were coming back," he whispered.

A beat.

"You lied."

'That door hadn't opened in a long time. Now, when it does, you're never on the other side.'

A pause.

'I can't claim that things are perfect. I can't claim that the gift you left me with is welcome. However, that gift. That lie. It's a beautiful one. Because in the end, it's all I've got left.'

Leland awoke with a stiff neck. He was surprised he'd fallen asleep here, of all places. His head had been hanging over the back of the couch when consciousness eventually returned.

"Well," he muttered. "That was different."

He shifted. It was then that he recalled he wasn't alone.

Leland sat in the quiet of the living room, the dim light from a nearby lamp casting soft shadows on the walls. Morgan was curled up on his lap, her small body trembling with the remnants of the earlier scare. He rocked her gently, murmuring soft reassurances, though his own heart was heavy. She had made it clear that getting her to bed alone tonight wasn't going to happen. The fear still lingered in her wide, tearful eyes, and Leland couldn't bring himself to force her into her own bed. Not tonight.

Across the room, Catherine sat on the edge of the couch, watching them. She was quiet, her hands folded in her lap, her gaze fixed on her father and sister. The distance between them was palpable, and Leland could feel the weight of her unspoken thoughts pressing against him. He knew she was still hurting from the morning's incident, from the way he had kept his distance all day. She had tried to bridge the gap, but he had pushed her away—physically and emotionally.

Leland wasn't ignorant of her gaze, nor of the tension that now sat heavily between them. He could feel it as keenly as the small, warm weight of Morgan on his lap. He looked down at his youngest daughter, still nestled against him, and then back at Catherine. The realization hit him with the force of a blow: he had been absent from her life too, even when he was physically present. The distance he had created today was just another example of the disconnect that had been growing between them since Helen's death.

With a heavy sigh, Leland knew he couldn't let it continue. He couldn't leave Catherine to navigate her pain alone. He shifted Morgan slightly, making room beside him, and reached out to Catherine. She hesitated for a moment, her eyes flicking to his hand, then to his face, searching for something—some sign that he truly wanted her there.

"Come here, Cat," Leland said softly, his voice thick with emotion. He pulled her closer to his side and draped an arm around her. She stiffened at first, but then slowly relaxed into his embrace, resting her head on his shoulder.

As they sat there together, Leland's thoughts drifted back over the day. He had tried, he really had, to be there for them. But the truth was, he hadn't been present at all. His body might have been with them, but his mind had been elsewhere—lost in a haze of grief, guilt, and regret. He had gone through the motions, but he hadn't truly connected with his daughters. Today was a perfect example of how his absence, even when he was physically there, was affecting them all.

Leland looked down at Morgan, her breathing starting to even out as she began to doze in his lap, and then at Catherine, still leaning against him. He pressed a kiss to the top of Catherine's head, his heart aching with the knowledge that he had failed them both. He couldn't change the past, but maybe—just maybe—he could start to make things right.

Leland rocked Morgan gently, her small frame nestled against him as she slowly drifted off to sleep. The weight of the day pressed heavily on him, but for the first time in what felt like an eternity, he allowed himself to simply be present with his daughters. Catherine leaned into his side, her quiet presence both a comfort and a reminder of the distance he had created between them. He pressed a kiss to the top of her head, trying to reassure her with the warmth of his embrace.

The room was silent except for the soft sound of Morgan's breathing and the distant hum of the house settling for the night. Leland's thoughts raced as he reflected on the day—on the mistakes he had made, the emotional walls he had built, and the unspoken pain that lingered between them all. He had gone through the motions for so long, but now, sitting here with his daughters, he realized how much he had missed.

From the corner of his eye, Leland noticed a shadow moving in the hallway. He looked up just as Angelina stepped into the room, her expression torn between hesitation and resolve. She paused in the doorway, watching her father and sisters with a mixture of longing and uncertainty. Leland's heart ached at the sight of her—his oldest daughter, who had borne so much of the weight of their loss.

Angelina stood there, frozen in place, her eyes fixed on the scene before her. She wanted to join them, to be part of this fragile moment of connection, but her anger still simmered beneath the surface. She resented the distance her father had created, the way he had disappeared into his grief and left them all to fend for themselves. And yet, she couldn't deny the deep longing she felt to have him back in her life, fully present and engaged.

From Leland's perspective, he could see the conflict in her eyes. He didn't say anything, didn't want to push her one way or the other.

Instead, he simply held out his hand, offering her the choice to join them if she was ready.

For a long moment, Angelina stood there, her gaze shifting between her father's outstretched hand and the sleeping form of her youngest sister. The anger she felt clashed with the overwhelming need to feel her father's presence again. It was a battle that raged within her, tearing at her resolve.

Then, slowly, Angelina made her decision. She stepped forward, her movements tentative, and sat down on the opposite side of her father. She didn't lean into him like Catherine had, didn't offer any words of reconciliation. But she was there, close enough to be part of the group, close enough to be included.

Angelina sat stiffly on the edge of the couch, her eyes darting between her father and sisters. She could feel the tension in her own body, the way her muscles resisted the urge to relax. Her father's presence beside her felt both comforting and suffocating, a reminder of what she had lost and what she desperately wanted to regain.

The anger was still there, simmering just beneath the surface. She wanted to lash out, to demand answers, to make him see how much he had hurt them all by disappearing into his grief. But as she glanced at Morgan, peacefully sleeping in his arms, and Catherine, who seemed to have found some measure of peace in his embrace, Angelina couldn't bring herself to do it.

Instead, she let herself soften, just a little. She allowed herself to lean slightly toward him, feeling the warmth of his presence. It wasn't much, but it was a start—a small step toward healing the rift that had grown between them.

She didn't know if things would ever be the same again. But sitting here, with her father's silent invitation to join them, she realized that maybe—just maybe—there was a chance to rebuild what they had lost. It would take time, and it wouldn't be easy, but for the first time in a long while, Angelina allowed herself to hope.

Chapter 9

Leland paced the floor of his study, his phone pressed to his ear as the senior partner's voice droned on. An emergency meeting had been called, something urgent enough to disrupt his Sunday at home. He released a held breath as he ended the call, already feeling the pressure of leaving his family behind once again.

Stepping into the kitchen, he found Janet and the girls in the midst of preparing dinner—a meal she had suggested as a way to spend more time together, something to anchor them in the chaos. Leland had readily agreed, knowing the girls needed more than just his presence; they needed a connection he hadn't been able to provide lately. Janet, with her warmth and steadiness, had become that bridge, a reasonable solution to fill the gaps he had left.

Morgan was the first to notice the tension in his face. She stepped forward, her small form dwarfed by his presence. "Daddy, are you alright?" she asked softly, her wide eyes searching his for reassurance.

Leland forced a smile that never reached his eyes. "Yeah, sweetie bird. I'm alright," he replied, trying to keep his voice steady. "But Daddy has to go into the office for a bit."

Janet glanced up from the stove, her expression falling slightly. "But..." she started, her voice trailing off as she took in the scene. The tension in the room was palpable enough for even Morgan to sense. Janet exhaled and lowered her gaze for a moment before looking back at him. "Are they calling all the partners, or just the corporate personnel?"

"Corporate, for now," Leland answered, his tone resigned.

Janet nodded slowly, understanding why she hadn't been called in as well. Her specialty wasn't in corporate law, and it was clear this meeting was outside her domain. "Do you think it will take long?" she asked, though she already anticipated the answer.

Leland shrugged. He rubbed his temples. "I'm not sure. I'll try to get back as quickly as I can." He bent down to kiss Morgan on the head, offering her a small, weary smile. "I'll be back soon, sweetie bird."

With that, he turned and left the kitchen, his footsteps echoing through the quiet house. The promise to be back in time for dinner hung in the air, but even as he said it, doubts crept into his mind.

Now, standing in his office at the firm, Leland listened half-heartedly as his colleague droned on about the new client issue. His thoughts kept drifting back to the kitchen, to the disappointed looks on Catherine and Angelina's faces when he told them he had to leave. The weight of his absence settled heavily on his shoulders, and for the first time in a long while, he wondered if he was truly making the right choices.

After Leland left, the house fell into a deep, almost oppressive silence. The only sound was the soft hum of the air conditioning, battling against the relentless summer heat outside. Janet was in the kitchen, absently stirring a of soup on the stove, her mind elsewhere. The girls sat around the table, their attention divided between their phones and the sporadic conversation that had started and stopped several times over the past hour.

Morgan had been quietly observing Janet. She noticed the way Janet had looked at her father—the same way her mother used to look at him. The thought lingered in her mind until she couldn't hold back any longer. Her voice, small but determined, broke the silence as she looked up from the book she was pretending to read. "Do you like my daddy?"

Janet's hand froze on the spoon, and for a moment, she was at a loss for words. She glanced over at Catherine and Angelina, searching their faces for a clue as to what they were thinking. But both girls were watching her intently, waiting for her answer.

"I..." Janet hesitated, her usual composure slipping. She sighed, placing the spoon down and turning to face them fully. "Yes, Morgan. I like your dad. He's a good friend that I care about a lot."

Morgan seemed to process this, her brow furrowing as she considered Janet's words. She wasn't entirely convinced that Janet's answer matched the kind of "like" she had in mind. She was tempted to press further, but Angelina, who had been reading the room, gently interrupted with a soft touch on her sister's shoulder. "Let's not talk about that right now, sweetie bird. Okay?" Her voice was low, meant only for Morgan to hear.

Morgan nodded, accepting the simple honesty in Janet's voice for now. But Catherine wasn't as easily swayed. Her gaze remained fixed on Janet, sharp and probing. "It's more than that, isn't it?" she asked, her directness catching Angelina off guard, who had been trying to steer the conversation away from anything too awkward.

Janet looked off to the side, unable to meet Catherine's piercing gaze. "Yes, it is," she admitted quietly. "But I've never tried to replace your mother. I could never... Helen was an amazing woman, and I know how much she meant to all of you. But she's not here anymore, and..."

Janet's voice trailed off as she searched for the right words, feeling the moment as something more than just light. She felt out of place, unsure of how to express her feelings without giving the impression that she was trying to take Helen's place in their lives. The last thing she wanted was for them to think she was overstepping boundaries that were still so fragile.

Angelina, who had been silent up until this point, finally spoke, her voice soft but steady. "You've been here for us when he couldn't be. And I know you care about us too. It's just... don't worry about it."

Janet nodded, understanding the weight of Angelina's words. "Alright. I'll keep that in mind," she said gently. "I'm here if you guys ever need me."

A brief silence followed, thick with unspoken feelings hanging in the air like a heavy fog. The tension only broke when Catherine glanced at the clock on the wall. "Dinner's almost ready. Should we set the table?" she asked, her tone brisk but carrying a hint of her usual composure.

Janet gave a small nod and smiled. "Yes, let's do that."

As the girls moved around the kitchen, preparing for dinner, Janet allowed herself a quiet, hopeful smile. The conversation wasn't over—not by a long shot—but it was a start. There was still a lot left unsaid, but at least they had begun to acknowledge it.

By the time Leland wrapped up the emergency meeting and rushed home, dinner was already on the table. The girls had eaten in near silence, their eyes drifting to the empty chair at the head of the table every few minutes. Morgan had been the first to break the quiet, asking Janet when their daddy would be back. Janet had reassured her that he'd be home soon, but the mood in the room lingered, thick and oppressive.

When Leland finally walked into the dining room, mere moments later, the atmosphere didn't lighten. His steps were slow, heavy with exhaustion, and smile he offered didn't settle on him just right. "I'm sorry I'm late," he said quietly as he took his seat at the table.

"It's alright," Janet replied, feeling it was her place to offer some reassurance.

Angelina shot a hard, almost scrutinizing look at her father. Her eyes shimmered with unshed tears, though she turned away too quickly for Leland to be sure. She focused intently on her plate, suddenly finding it the most fascinating thing in the world.

Leland noticed the tension in her movements, the way her hands gripped the utensils just a bit too tightly. He knew something was brewing beneath the surface, something he hadn't yet confronted, but the exhaustion in his bones made it hard to reach out—to push past the barriers that had formed between them.

For now, all he could do was eat in silence and hope that, somehow, he could find a way to make things right.

A presence hung over the dining room table—not empty, but dense with meaning none of them could quite grasp. Still, it pressed down on them all the same. The cause lingered just out of reach—an unspoken tension they all felt but couldn't define.

Catherine, ever the one trying to keep things together, broke the silence first. "You know, this soup is really good, Janet. You're a great cook."

Janet smiled at the compliment, grateful for the attempt to lighten the mood. "Thank you, Catherine. I'm glad you like it."

Angelina glanced at her sister, noticing the subtle effort Catherine was making to lift the atmosphere. A pang of guilt pricked at her, realizing she hadn't done the same. Catherine had always been the one to try to hold things together, even when everything seemed to be falling apart. It was a role she had taken on without anyone asking her to, and Angelina knew the weight of it must be exhausting.

Determined to help her sister out and break the unbearable silence, Angelina started talking. She engaged in conversation with her sisters and Janet, bringing up any and every topic she could think of. Her voice filled the room more than Leland could remember hearing in recent months, her words an attempt to keep the darkness at bay.

But as dinner progressed, the fragile conversation began to unravel. The girls' disappointment in their father's earlier absence, Leland's continued detachment, and Janet's mounting frustration all simmered beneath the surface, threatening to boil over. Catherine, still trying to keep the conversation flowing, eventually made a comment about how nice it would be to resume their Sunday dinners—a tradition they had abandoned since Helen's passing. Her voice wavered slightly as she fought to maintain her composure.

"I miss when we all used to sit down together like this," Catherine said, trying to sound casual but failing to hide the crack in her voice. "It felt... normal."

Leland glanced up from his plate, hearing the tremor in her words. The strain in her eyes was unmistakable, and he could see the toll that trying to hold everything together had taken on her. She had grown so much, he realized, stepping into a role she should never have had to fill. The bitter realization that she was cracking under the pressure hit him hard, forcing him to confront just how much he had been absent—physically and emotionally—from their lives.

Morgan stood up from her seat, her small frame moving quietly as she pushed her chair away from the table. She kept her eyes fixed on the ground, shuffling slowly to her father's side. Leland placed his fork down, a look of surprise crossing his face as he watched her approach. She stood there, frozen like a wooden marionette, waiting. He gently pushed back from the table, making enough room for Morgan to climb into his lap.

All eyes turned to Leland as he sat there, arms limp and lifeless as he awkwardly draped them around his daughter. Morgan's head found its way onto his shoulder, seeking comfort. The conversation faltered. The moment stretched, the disconnect heavier with every passing second.

Janet, who had been watching Leland closely, finally reached her breaking point. She had seen this detachment before—the same distance that had plagued him for a while—and she couldn't hold back any longer.

"Leland, I'm getting sick of this," she began, her voice tight with barely suppressed anger, "I know you loved Helen. I know how much you were invested in your relationship with her. But she's gone, Leland. It's been *years* since she passed. *Not* months. *Not* days." Her voice wavered as frustration seeped into every word. "I've been trying to help you and the girls, to be there for all of you..." Her voice softened, nearly breaking as she added, "And *I've* been here. Waiting..."

Leland looked up, startled by the intensity of her words. The room fell into an uneasy silence, her confession hanging in the air like a weight no one could ignore.

Janet took a deep breath, steadying herself. She tapped her chest for emphasis as she continued, "I'm not trying to replace her, Leland. I could never do that. But I'm here. I care about you... About all of you." Her words were raw, vulnerable, the unspoken truth clear to everyone—even Morgan, who clung tighter to her father. "But if you can't move forward... I don't know how much longer I can keep doing this."

Tears brimmed at the corners of Janet's eyes as she spoke, her emotions laid bare.

A small movement drew Leland's attention back to Morgan. He looked down to see that she, too, had started crying—silent tears streaming down her cheeks as her tiny shoulders hitched with suppressed sobs.

The confession hung, raw and unresolved. Angelina and Catherine exchanged glances, their expressions shifting from surprise to understanding. They had seen how much Janet had been there for them when their father couldn't be. And now, they realized just how deeply she cared—not just for them, but for their father as well.

Catherine was the first to speak, her voice quiet but resolute. "She's right, Dad. We can't keep living in the past. We need you here... with us."

Morgan, still sniffling, added softly between sobs, "I like Janet. She's nice. And she makes you smile, Daddy."

In the small silence that followed, Leland's gaze drifted to his oldest daughter, Angelina. Everyone else had spoken. He wondered what she thought, what she held inside. His voice, barely more than a whisper, seemed even quieter than the hush in the room, as if the stillness itself could almost drown it out.

"What about you?"

Angelina remained silent, her emotions churning inside her. She had been holding onto her resentment for so long, feeling disconnected from her father. But now, seeing him sitting there, confronted by Janet's words and her sisters' quiet support, something inside her broke.

The tears came suddenly, spilling over before she could stop them. "I need you, Dad," she choked out, her voice shaking. "I've been so angry at you, and I've tried to be strong, but I can't do this on my own. I need you to be *here* with *us*. I need you to be my *dad*."

Her breakdown was sudden and raw, the emotions she had buried for so long finally spilling out. Leland reached out, pulling her into his arms, holding her tightly as she cried.

"I'm so sorry, Angel," he whispered, his own tears falling. "I'm so sorry."

Eventually, Catherine came around the table to give her father a hug as well.

As he held his girls, Leland felt the shift—something inside him finally breaking free. He realized that it wasn't just about surviving anymore. It was about being there for them, about moving forward, not just for himself but for his daughters. For Janet. For all of them.

The girls gathered around him, their arms wrapping around him in a protective embrace. Leland felt their warmth, their love, and in that moment, he knew he had to change. He couldn't keep living in the shadow of his grief. He had to move forward, for them.

Janet watched from across the table, her own emotions raw and exposed. But as she saw the family come together, her feelings lifted slightly. She had spoken her truth, and now it was up to Leland to take the next step. She drew in a breath—not from weariness, but release.

And as the night wore on, there was a sense of hope in the air—a quiet, fragile hope that maybe, just maybe, they could all start to heal. Leland took it all in. His thoughts no longer colored in subdued shades.

No longer dark, but not bright. Not yet—just open.

'I've been grieving the loss so long, I forgot how to see what's still here.'

He turned and smiled gently at Janet. She, hesitant, returned it readily.

"I'll try. With you," he mouthed to her.

"Thank you," she returned, eyes brimming with tears. The girls were unaware of the exchange.

By Innocence Commanded

Chapter 1

The castle stood like a crown upon the high cliffs, its pale stone glowing faintly beneath the soft touch of morning light. From the horizon, hills rose and fell like gentle waves—rolling fields of wheat swayed in rhythm with the breeze. Beyond, scattered villages lay nestled against the hills, their thatched rooftops still catching the lingering mist.

Closer, the city proper unfolded: orderly streets and clustered stone buildings nestled beneath the protection of the towering castle walls. And closer still—within those walls—the open veranda extended like a terrace above the world.

Here, beneath a white canvas awning fluttering lazily, a modest table had been prepared. Silver trays glinted in the morning light. Fresh bread still steamed beside carved fruits and delicate cuts of cheese. A crystal decanter held watered wine, and the faint aroma of roasted nuts lingered.

Leonid, not yet fourteen, sat alone for the moment, dressed not in royal formality but in simple robes of deep blue. Only the faintest threading of gold embroidery along the cuffs and collar betrayed his station. The breeze toyed gently with the loose ends of his sleeves.

He waited.

His hand rested lightly around the slender stem of a goblet. His eyes wandered past the city rooftops, past the fields, toward the distant hills.

Behind him, the soft shuffle of slippers across smooth stone announced her approach.

"Forgive me," came her voice, light as a song. "I didn't mean to keep you waiting."

Leonid turned with a small smile as Isolde emerged fully into view. Isolde had only seen twelve summers, but there was a certain natural poise in her that made her seem older in fleeting moments.

She crossed the veranda with easy grace, her light summer gown catching the morning air as she moved. Her hair, the color of warm honey, was drawn back loosely. No jewelry. No formal wear. Just simple, effortless beauty.

"You're never late," Leonid said softly. "When you arrive, the day begins."

She returned his smile and slipped into the seat across from him. The single servant nearby—a quiet woman in gray livery—stepped forward to refill the goblet and pour another for Isolde before retreating a respectful distance.

The pair settled into a rhythm familiar to them both.

They spoke quietly at first, of nothing at all. The weather. The coming harvest. The birdsong that filled the air. At one point, Leonid tore off a piece of warm bread, handed it across the table. She accepted it with an impish grin, as though they were playing at some private ritual.

"I think your castle pigeons are growing fat," Isolde said, glancing toward the stone rail where several birds had perched. "Perhaps they've grown lazy under your rule."

Leonid chuckled lightly. "Then they reflect their king well."

"Hmm." She tapped her chin playfully. "I don't recall you being so lazy last night."

A small flush colored his cheeks. He glanced sideways at the servant, but the woman remained respectfully distant, eyes lowered. Isolde laughed softly, pleased with her little victory.

They continued like this—drifting through idle conversation, teasing, and quiet smiles beneath the rising sun.

As the meal neared its end, Isolde rose and wandered toward the edge of the veranda, gazing out over the land spread below. Her fingers traced the cool marble of the balustrade.

Leonid watched her for a time, his expression softening.

"My father used to say," she mused, "that one could see all the kingdom's hope from this balcony. I think he was only partly right."

"Oh?"

She turned, her smile smaller now, but no less sincere.

"The hope of a land rests here," she said softly, tapping her fingertips against his chest. "Here, my king."

Leonid caught her hand gently. "Then I shall hold it carefully."

Their eyes met, held, then parted again in comfortable silence.

At last, she excused herself, promising to meet him later near the gardens for their afternoon ride. Her departing footsteps whispered away, leaving the terrace bathed once more in tranquil quiet.

Leonid remained seated as the servant cleared the table with efficiency.

The goblet remained in his hand. He lifted it, sipping lightly, his gaze once again drifting outward across the land.

The breeze sighed against the marble columns. The city rooftops gleamed beneath the advancing sun. Beyond them, the golden fields rippled softly like a living sea.

And Leonid sat alone, quietly sipping his wine.

The sun had climbed well past its morning slant, now filtering soft brilliance through the arched windows of Leonid's private apartments. The air carried the faintest fragrance of crushed lavender — lingering from the bundles the maids had tucked discreetly into the corners earlier. Sheer curtains stirred gently in the warm breeze that slipped past the stone lattice.

The royal apartments hummed with quiet activity.

Two chambermaids worked silently near the far wall, folding and replacing linens. A steward checked inventory at the sideboard, adjusting the arrangement of decanters and polished silver with deft precision. A pair of young pages passed through the entry, carrying fresh water and lightly perfumed cloths.

Leonid stood near the tall mirror set against the interior wall, watching the room's movements reflected in glass. He idly adjusted the gold-threaded sash draped across his deep green riding tunic. The garment was light, tailored for ease of movement, though its fine stitching betrayed wealth. His fingers traced the edge absentmindedly.

The reflection shifted as his valet approached.

"Your Highness," the man said with a small bow of his head, "the preparations are nearly complete."

The valet—Alden—was a lean man, not yet thirty, with sharp eyes that missed very little. His voice always carried a careful balance of deference and familiarity, knowing well his position as Leonid's most regular attendant since childhood.

"Alden," Leonid began. He fidgeted at the high collar beneath his sash. "Can't I wear something less... stiff?" he whined.

Alden looked at Leonid carefully.

"Why, Your Highness? You look rather handsome."

Leonid lightly tugged at the garment again.

"But it's so damn... uncomfortable."

Alden glanced nervously over his shoulder before quickly turning back to Leonid.

"Your Highness, you can't talk like that, it's unbecoming of a man in your station." Alden reached over and gently pulled Leonid's hands away from the collar, smoothing the material immediately afterwards.

Leonid grimaced loudly.

"And besides," Alden continued as if Leonid hadn't moaned. "You have to dress the part of the monarch you are," he smiled.

Leonid nodded once, glancing toward the set of riding gloves laid neatly on the side table. "Thank you, Alden."

The valet stepped closer, his hands already beginning their practiced adjustments. With gentle precision, he straightened the folds of the sash and brushed away an invisible speck from Leonid's shoulder. The faint scent of fresh wool and leather oil drifted faintly from the garments waiting by the rack.

"You enjoyed your morning, I hope?" Alden asked, voice mild as his hands continued their work.

Leonid smiled faintly. "It was... pleasant."

"Lady Isolde seemed in fine spirits when she departed the gardens earlier," Alden offered with an almost playful tone. "The servants say you spent much of the morning beneath the plum trees."

"We did." Leonid's smile widened slightly, his gaze growing distant as memory crept in. "She found a little green frog and insisted it was a prince in hiding."

Alden gave a soft chuckle. "A most merciful young lady to offer such charity to frogs."

Leonid exhaled softly, his eyes lowering for a moment. "She makes it easy to forget... everything else."

Alden paused his movements for a heartbeat. "That is what youth should be, Your Highness."

Leonid's expression shifted—just a flicker. The loss of his father, only a year past, still bothered him. But it faded as quickly as it surfaced.

The valet lifted the dark riding cloak from the rack and draped it over Leonid's shoulders. The polished clasp clicked softly into place beneath his collar.

"The horses are being readied as we speak. Sir Calwin awaits your arrival in the courtyard. And the Lady has requested her favorite white mare be saddled."

"Good." Leonid inhaled deeply. "The lake should be beautiful this afternoon."

"Indeed, Your Highness." Alden stepped back a pace, surveying his young king. "If I may say... this weather seems made for young hearts."

Leonid laughed softly—not forced, but genuine. "You may say it, Alden."

For a moment, they stood together in companionable silence.

Then Alden added, his voice dropping slightly more formal again, "Shall I alert the guards to escort you to the stables?"

Leonid gave a small shake of his head. "No. Let them remain discreet today. There are enough eyes in the castle already."

Alden dipped his head in acknowledgment. "Very well, sire."

As Leonid turned toward the broad doorway leading into the marble hall beyond, a faint hum of garden birds drifted in through the open windows. The castle, for now, held its breath — as though time itself offered the boy-king one more afternoon untouched by politics, unrest, or consequence.

And so he went, leaving the light chatter of the servants behind as they continued their quiet orchestration within his chamber.

The afternoon sun hovered warm above the countryside, its light bending gently through drifting clouds as Isolde and Leonid rode side by side along the narrow trail. Beyond them, golden fields bowed with the wind, as if offering respect to the young monarch and his lady. All the while, the faint murmur of distant birdsong carried in brief waves across the open air.

Their horses moved at an easy gait—his tall black stallion steady beneath him, her smaller white mare prancing with light steps, ears flicking at every whisper of wind.

The castle had faded far behind, its towering spires reduced to distant markers beyond the rolling hills. The lake lay ahead—hidden behind a thin ridge of trees, but close now.

For a while, they rode in comfortable silence, broken only by the occasional snort from one of the animals or a passing comment on the countryside.

"You promised to take me rowing again," Isolde said suddenly, flashing him a teasing glance.

Leonid smiled. "And I will. If you promise not to try and race me this time."

She gave an exaggerated gasp. "I nearly won, you know."

"That is... generous of you to believe."

The trail narrowed briefly as they passed between two high banks. The thick grasses swayed heavily along the periphery of the path. Leonid glanced toward her again, admiring how the sun caught her hair like honeyed silk.

And then it happened.

From the brush ahead, a low rustle cut through the stillness. A long, slender shadow writhed out into the dirt trail—a large snake, startled by the horses.

Isolde's white mare reared sharply with a panicked shriek, hooves pawing the air. The sudden motion threw her body forward, and for a moment her balance wavered. The horse spun half-sideways, muscles coiling in fright.

Leonid saw it—belatedly. His eyes had been upon her face rather than the ground. The sudden lurch pulled him upright in alarm.

"Isolde!"

But before he could even fully react, she was already drawing the reins tight. Her voice came firm, steady—not a scream but a sharp command to the animal beneath her.

"Steady—steady!"

The mare tossed once more, hooves scraping the loose dirt, but Isolde held firm. She leaned low, coaxing, guiding, refusing to surrender control.

Within moments, the animal stilled beneath her hands. Its sides heaved, nostrils flaring, but it obeyed. She kept her head high, breathing hard but focused. The snake had already vanished into the grass.

Leonid pulled alongside her now, his stallion holding its ground easily. His face, however, was pale.

"Are you hurt?" he asked, voice tight with concern.

"No," she answered softly, her breathing slowing. "I'm fine."

But still he reached, his hand brushing over her arm, then up to her shoulder—an unconscious need to reassure himself. She allowed the touch, meeting his gaze with quiet steadiness.

"You handled her well," he said. His voice wanted to be strong, but there was something fragile under it.

Her lips curved faintly. "Of course I did."

He let his hand linger a second longer before lowering it, drawing in a breath of relief.

Neither spoke of it, but both felt the unspoken truth passing between them.

The moment had shaken him far more than her.

And she knew.

The tumult had drawn the attention of their small accompaniment — the few knights Leonid had allowed to ride with them. Two knights pulled up short beside them.

"Your Highness, are you alright?"

Leonid looked at him curiously.

His gaze flicked past the knight toward Isolde—not in confusion, but in brief irritation.

The knight, like any loyal guard, had done as trained: protect the sovereign above all else.

But it hadn't been his life in danger.

Isolde caught his eye and offered the smallest shake of her head, her expression soft but steady—a quiet reminder: duty, not disrespect.

Leonid exhaled through his nose and waved a hand dismissively.

"I'm fine."

He glanced at the rest of the company: two other knights not far behind, waiting for orders from their captain. Isolde's Lady-in-waiting watched anxiously, though she remained at the appropriate distance, giving the young pair privacy without abandoning propriety.

"Have your men ride ahead and ensure the trail is clear. The lake is not much farther," said Leonid.

He drew closer to Isolde, took her reins, and helped her slip sidesaddle in front of him onto his horse. He slipped his arms around her waist and held her close.

She allowed his comfort not because she needed it, but because he did.

And though no words passed between them, they both knew: it was not her fear he was soothing—it was her soothing his own by her presence and submission.

The lake shimmered beneath the afternoon light, its surface dappled with gold as small ripples played across the water. Thin reeds swayed gently at the edges, while dragonflies darted and hovered in quiet bursts of movement. The air smelled faintly of warm grass and distant blossoms carried on the breeze.

Leonid rowed with steady, measured strokes, guiding the small boat smoothly across the shallows. Opposite him, Isolde sat cross-legged on the narrow bench, her slippers neatly tucked beneath her as she watched the water trail behind them. The delicate lace hem of her gown brushed lightly against the wooden floorboards.

Leonid smiled inwardly as he looked back at the shore. He had thought he would have to fight to keep a knight from accompanying him and insisting on rowing the boat. Had Alden been there, it would have been impossible. But he had won at in the end. The privilege of the crown, one could say.

The single Lady-in-waiting permitted to accompany them waited dutifully in the shade as Leonid guided the boat alone.

For several moments they drifted in companionable silence, the boat rocking gently with the pull of the oars.

"Look!" she suddenly exclaimed, pointing toward the far shore. "Another frog prince, no doubt."

Leonid followed her gaze, spotting a plump green frog perched boldly on a lily pad.

"I didn't know I had so many brothers," Leonid said dryly.

Isolde stuck her tongue out.

"You do seem determined to see royalty in every puddle and pond," he teased.

"Perhaps I should collect them," she answered with a grin. "In case this one turns unworthy, I shall have backups."

He shook his head with a smile, easing the oars to let them drift freely. "I fear for my throne."

Isolde giggled and shifted playfully, extending her bare foot toward the cool water. As she leaned forward to tap the surface, one of her slippers slipped loose and tumbled dangerously close to the edge.

With a surprised squeak, she caught it just in time, laughing as she fell back onto the bench.

Leonid laughed with her, his voice light and easy.

"Careful, my Lady. You'll have your slipper swimming next."

"Then you would be forced to retrieve it, and I doubt you'd let me hear the end of it."

Their laughter drifted across the still water, fading beneath the hum of insects and distant birds.

Soon, as the sun began its slow descent toward evening, the boat returned to shore, and their small party prepared for the ride back toward the castle.

By twilight, the castle's great dining hall glowed softly beneath warm lantern light. The long table, dressed in fine linen, stretched beneath banners of deep blue and gold. Servants moved like shadows between the courses, setting fresh platters of roasted game and honeyed fruits.

Leonid and Isolde sat together near the head of the table, though the space around them remained respectfully unfilled. They dined alone. This meal was not for court, nor council, but for the young lord and his closest companion.

They spoke little, both content in the easy rhythm of shared glances and quiet smiles. Occasionally, Leonid passed her a sweet from his plate, which she accepted with theatrical grace, as though gifted some grand royal favor.

Their private world held steady beneath the steady clatter of silver and the soft murmur of attending servants.

Later, as evening deepened and stars began to prick the sky, Leonid escorted Isolde through the long marbled corridor toward her chambers. The halls lay quiet, tall candelabras casting slow-moving shadows along the walls.

They walked without hurry.

At her door, she turned toward him, her eyes reflecting the flickering flame nearby.

"Don't stay up late thinking too much again," she whispered with a small smile.

He returned her gaze and gently took her hand, pressing a brief kiss to her knuckles. "Not tonight."

The heavy oak door creaked softly as it opened, and she slipped inside with one final glance back.

Leonid stood for a moment longer, watching as the door closed behind her. The castle settled once again into stillness, the hum of crickets filling the quiet corridors.

He exhaled slowly and turned away, his footsteps echoing softly into the deepening night.

Chapter 2

A somewhat quiet year passed. Now, the great hall buzzed with muted conversation beneath vaulted ceilings of pale stone. Sunlight streamed through tall windows, casting patterned light across the polished marble floor where noblemen and courtiers gathered in loose clusters.

Leonid stood near the center dais, dressed in simple formal attire — still modest by royal standards, but cut with just enough elegance to command presence. The banners of his house hung behind him, deep blue silk embroidered with the golden stag that marked his lineage.

Isolde stood at his side, her hand lightly resting on his arm. She wore pale green, the fabric flowing like water around her, her honey-colored hair gathered into loose braids that framed her face with youthful softness.

"My Lord King," came a warm voice, approaching with careful precision.

Duke Eldric—a distant cousin of Leonid, and father to Isolde—bowed with a dignity that was neither exaggerated nor perfunctory. His face bore the lines of experience but carried a softness in the eyes whenever they fell upon his daughter.

"My daughter sings praises of your mornings together," he said with a small smile. "She speaks of you, sire, as if you hung the stars by hand."

Leonid offered a quiet chuckle.

"If only I had such power."

Isolde smiled but said nothing. Her fingers gently squeezed his arm.

Leonid reached over and patted her hand.

"Would you like to own a star?" he asked softly.

Isolde gently reached up. Her fingers brushed Leonid's cheek. She leaned a bit closer, intent on keeping propriety while staying close enough to conceal her words, and said, "and what good would that do me? I've something better here."

She leaned back, raising a kerchief to her mouth to cover her blush. Leonid, however, was tempted to move the kerchief aside and place a kiss on her lips in response to her words. He held back, knowing it might cause scandal. They hadn't wed just yet, despite the date fast approaching.

From the side, Duke Eldric watched the interaction. Silently. His expression unreadable.

Nearby footsteps caused Leonid to return his gaze to those gathered.

From the side, Chancellor Reginald approached with his usual quiet gravity. The older man bowed, though his expression remained measured.

"Your Majesty," Reginald began softly, "the preparations for the upcoming festival proceed on schedule. The city's mood is... expectant."

Leonid nodded. "Good. The people deserve some joy after this past year."

Reginald hesitated for half a breath. "Indeed, sire. Though... there are small matters of protocol being raised by certain families. Requests for specific seating privileges, ceremonial honors, participation in the opening rites. Nothing urgent yet."

Duke Eldric exhaled with a knowing sigh. "The noble houses do love to remind one another who carries the heavier purse."

Leonid's gaze shifted between them both. "And they shall be indulged—within reason."

The Chancellor bowed again. "As you command."

The atmosphere remained light, but the undertone was undeniable: politics lived even beneath festivities.

One of the court stewards approached, whispering briefly to Reginald. The Chancellor gave a small nod of dismissal, then turned back toward Leonid with a barely audible murmur: "The Uriliation priests have secured a small corner of the merchant district for their procession. It's... grown modestly larger than last year."

Duke Eldric's brow furrowed, but he spoke nothing aloud. Leonid's smile never wavered.

"Let them have their corner," Leonid said. "The kingdom allows many voices, Chancellor."

"As you wish," Reginald answered, though his tone carried a hint of unease.

Isolde glanced at Leonid briefly, sensing the faint shift beneath the surface—but neither of them spoke further on it. This was not the moment.

Duke Eldric cleared his throat gently, to get the attention of his Lord.

"Speak, cousin," Leonid said.

Eldric looked towards his daughter first, then Leonid. "Have you considered my proposal?" he asked.

Leonid first rose a brow. It was Reginald who responded.

"Lord Eldric," he began. "The wedding cannot be advanced before the coming of age ceremony. Our traditions have held firm in this regard for centuries."

Reginald glanced between Isolde and Leonid, gauging her reaction to her father's renewed proposal, and his Lord's response to the maneuver behind it. This glance, however, was to gauge how Leonid would respond to the threads of power positioning that lay underneath such a request.

Leonid's expression revealed nothing. As if the question hadn't even been asked. As if he was unaware of the maneuvering. An earlier wedding would allow the Duke to gain more standing amongst the gentry. He seemed to want to get this as soon as possible, not wanting to wait a mere few months more.

Eldric, displeased that the Chancellor had deflected his inquiry, gave a respectful bow and moved off without another word.

Leonid turned his head slightly towards Isolde, his eyes still locked on the retreating Duke.

"Your father wants to use you to increase his influence. You do know that, don't you?"

Isolde patted Leonid's hand. She kept her eyes fixed on her father.

"Your will is my will," she said softly.

That, and nothing more.

The smile that fitted her face, although beautiful, was a mask. A court trick. Used to diffuse, in this moment, those who may have noticed the spark that had occurred. There was no mirth or joy behind it, but no one besides Leonid would have been able to tell the difference.

The distant bells rang twice, signaling the midday hour. Another steward arrived, announcing the start of the next meeting with the guild leaders. Leonid sighed softly and offered his arm more firmly to Isolde.

"Come," he said with a private smile, "let us remind the merchants that even trade bends to charm."

Isolde's eyes sparkled. "Then you may rely upon me entirely."

As they moved toward the council chamber, the nobles behind them exchanged brief murmurs — too quiet for royal ears — but not lost upon Reginald, whose thoughtful eyes lingered a moment longer than necessary.

A week later, the festival opened beneath a cloudless sky. Bright banners stretched from high towers, their vibrant colors rippling in the breeze as laughter and music filled the wide stone plaza at the heart of the capital. Merchants called out from their stalls. Children wove through the crowds, chasing ribbons and sweets. The scent of roasted meats and spiced honey floated through the warm air.

Isolde stood at Leonid's side beneath the central pavilion. Their respective entourages—knights, advisors, attendants, and Isolde's Ladies-in-waiting—lingered at careful distance, allowing them a pocket of privacy amid the jubilant throng.

Leonid glanced back at his valet, Alden, and gave him a smile. It had been a significant challenge to get even this much freedom from close escort, let alone agreement that he could be near the actual festivities.

The nobles had balked at the idea, but Leonid pressed on, wondering who, actually, was the sovereign. At one point, he'd remarked darkly to Isolde, "What's the use in being a king if I can't even do what I want?" She'd only laughed lightly in response.

Leonid's formal attire bore only modest regalia: deep blue silks with narrow threads of gold at his collar and cuffs, enough to signify his station but not overwhelm. Beside him, Isolde wore pale violet, simple and elegant, her honeyed braids pinned loosely behind her shoulders. She glowed beneath the sun, her hand resting lightly in the crook of his arm.

"You planned this beautifully," Isolde whispered, eyes scanning the vibrant stalls around them.

Leonid's brow rose. "I had nothing to do with this. I did only what a leader is supposed to do," he said, then paused.

Isolde, knowing him, waited for him to continue without so much as giving a response to his quiet.

Leonid, defeated, chuckled lightly. "I delegated. I didn't actually plan anything."

"But still," she began gently, "you were instrumental because you pushed for this, despite the interference of the noble faction wanting to have a piece to show their power off. If they'd had their way, this would have taken another month to occur."

Leonid smiled faintly. "The people deserve something pleasant for once."

They strolled together through the square, the crowds parting naturally before them. Courtiers bowed with grace; children waved timidly. The air hummed with peaceful energy. For a time, it felt as though the world could truly remain like this—bright, simple, untouched.

A chant rose somewhere beyond the market's edge—faint at first, but growing louder.

Leonid's eyes narrowed. His knights stiffened instinctively.

Through the distant archways emerged a procession of robed priests—Uriliation followers. Their brown and crimson banners swayed as they advanced, chanting praises to their foreign god. Their flock followed close behind, dozens of commoners threading into the plaza—a bold move to interrupt the king's festival.

The surrounding citizens didn't take kindly to the intrusion. Angry murmurs spread quickly. A few shouts cut through the chant, challenging the priests' presence. The mood shifted—tension slipping like cold fingers between the bodies pressed together.

A commoner, a nondescript older man, appeared from the crowd. He, likely, taking it upon himself to be the representative leader of the opposition to the priests presence. His voice rang out over the chants.

"Go on. We don't want you here."

Others joined in. The chants became less coordinated as the voices rose.

"Yeah! Let us enjoy our festival. You've no right to be here!" came another voice from the gathering crowd of protesters.

Chancellor Reginald approached swiftly from the side, voice low but urgent.

"Your Majesty—you should withdraw to safety. We cannot predict—"

Leonid raised a hand. Slowly. Firmly.

"No," Leonid said calmly. "I remain here."

"But sire—"

Leonid looked behind him at the knights that seemed to vibrate with the intent to come to his side. He'd already given his order earlier. "Don't intrude on Isolde's and my space." That command choked them now.

He gave a subtle shake of his head to Alden and thrust his chin. Alden gathered the Ladies-in-waiting and then moved off towards the castle.

He then looked back to his Chancellor.

Leonid's voice remained even, almost gentle. "I will not retreat. I will not have the people believe that I value my own safety over theirs."

Reginald swallowed his protest, bowing his head. "As you command."

The crowd swelled with shouts now. Several citizens jostled against the encroaching priests. Someone threw a small piece of fruit—another retaliated by shoving back. A pocket of scuffling broke out on the far edge.

Looking at the captain, he gave a nod. The captain, understanding the silent command, motioned his men forward. The knights stepped forward, forming a firm line around Leonid and Isolde.

Leonid's gaze swept the gathering calmly. His hand brushed lightly against Isolde's back as if to steady her, though she hadn't moved.

"Captain," he said to his lead knight. "Form two lines between the two groups. Push back only as necessary to keep the center clear. No drawn swords unless commanded."

The orders rippled out efficiently. The knights moved into place, their shields forming a living barrier between the opposing groups. Raised voices continued to clash—angry peasants against zealous adherents—but no full violence yet. Only the volatile pressure of bodies pressing forward, daring the thin line to break. The priests stood in the background.

And then—

A rock flew.

Leonid's head snapped toward the motion. The stone arced wildly through the air, thrown by no one they could immediately see. It whistled past him—and past Isolde—missing her by barely a hand's width before striking the stone steps behind them with a sharp crack.

Isolde gasped softly—not from fear, but instinctive shock at the nearness. She clutched Leonid's arm tighter, her composure wavering for just a moment before settling once again. Her lips tightened. Her breath slowed deliberately. She did not cry out. She did not retreat. But her knuckles whitened around his sleeve.

Leonid never shifted his footing. His eyes scanned the gathered faces, registering everything, but his voice stayed cool.

"Disperse them," he said evenly to his captain.

With disciplined force, the knights advanced—shields held high, batons drawn to push rather than wound. The opposing groups slowly peeled apart under firm pressure. A few protestors stumbled, some shouted fresh insults, but no fresh violence erupted. The priests withdrew toward the edge of the square as their chant faltered.

Within minutes, the tension thinned. The crowd's angry energy dissolved into mutters and scattered curses as people reluctantly drifted away. The plaza emptied slowly but steadily.

Reginald's voice came from Leonid's side, opposite Isolde. "Your Majesty, I believe we may have to cancel—"

"We'll do no such thing," came Isolde's soft voice.

A moment of silence followed as all eyes, even those of nearby commoners, shifted to her.

"We'll continue the festival," she said steadily.

A spattering of applause broke out before cheers began ringing through the street.

Leonid waved his hand at the people. A smile fixed on his face. He nodded once more to the captain and watched as he commanded the knights to close ranks a bit tighter around the king.

Only then did Leonid turn fully toward Isolde, his mask lowering ever so slightly.

"Are you certain you're unharmed?" His voice dropped to a near whisper.

"I'm not hurt," she whispered back. "But... it came so close."

She drew a slow, deliberate breath—but her voice trembled at the edges now, the delayed weight finally pressing inward. She squeezed his arm again, searching his eyes not for reassurance, but to anchor herself.

"Come," Leonid said softly. "We return to the castle."

Isolde initially resisted.

"The festival will continue," Leonid reassured her softly.

With that reassurance, she finally gave in and let him lead her away.

His knights formed ranks around them as they moved away from the square. Boots thudded in synchrony, reverberating off the shopfronts lining the road. Light dust arose.

Shortly afterwards, they reached the castle. Alden was there to greet the king and stood ready if he was needed.

Confident in their security, Leonid dismissed everyone. The Ladies-in-waiting, who had also gathered at their arrival, initially seemed to protest but a quick look from Leonid subdued them.

The gaze held no anger.

Nor was it an attempt at bargaining.

It was resolute. There would be no question of the dismissal. They inevitably acquiesced, bowed and moved off as well.

Leonid slipped his arm into Isolde's and led her further in the castle.

Only when they reached the safety of Leonid's private chambers did the final shield fall.

As the doors closed behind them, Isolde exhaled sharply and allowed herself to tremble, just slightly. She gripped his tunic as though it were the only solid thing remaining beneath her.

Leonid wrapped his arms fully around her, holding her close, lowering his head against hers.

"It's over," he whispered. "You are safe."

Her breath caught once in her throat, but she steadied herself, pressing into his embrace.

"I wasn't frightened... until I thought of you," she whispered softly.

"And then..." she said haltingly. "And then I couldn't stop seeing it happen."

Leonid held her tighter, his eyes closed now as his restraint dissolved in private.

"You don't have to be strong here," he whispered.

She nodded faintly against his chest. She had to admit that while she'd been more afraid of Leonid coming to harm, her own safety and the possibility of injury had scared her as well.

She took a deep breath and released it slowly. Together they stood, quiet in the flickering candlelight, both letting down what they dared not reveal before others.

The council chamber was smaller than the grand halls but no less elegant. Sunlight streamed through tall windows of stained glass, casting muted colors across the polished marble floor. The banners of the royal house hung behind Leonid's seat, their golden stag gleaming in the morning light.

The room carried a different tone today — not celebratory, but watchful.

A small assembly had gathered. Duke Eldric sat quietly to one side, his expression composed, hands folded on his knee. Three other minor lords filled the remaining seats along the crescent-shaped table, their faces attentive but silent for now.

At Leonid's immediate right stood Chancellor Reginald.

Isolde was absent, as expected. Officially, she was resting after the disturbance the day before. Privately, she had yielded to Leonid's request, allowing him to manage today's affairs without her.

Leonid sat with perfect posture, hands resting lightly on the carved arms of his chair, his youthful features composed beneath the subtle weight that now hung in the air.

Reginald stepped forward slightly, voice steady but heavy with concern.

"Your Majesty... yesterday's incident—though contained—demands attention."

Leonid's eyes shifted toward him. "Speak plainly, Chancellor."

Reginald inclined his head. "The Uriliation priests have grown bolder with each passing season. They use our tolerance as cover to spread their influence deeper among the common folk. Yesterday's intrusion was not simply a misstep of zeal. It was intentional, Your Majesty. A provocation."

Leonid let the words settle a moment. "Provocation, perhaps. But not yet treason."

"Not yet," Reginald agreed quietly. "But their numbers increase. Their processions grow larger. And their rhetoric... shifts. They speak not only of their god but of leaders more aligned with their vision for this realm."

Leonid's gaze was steady. "The kingdom recognizes no official religion. All are free to worship."

"Until that worship becomes a means of political subversion," Reginald pressed, his tone tightening. "Their faith comes from across the border, from a land where religion and rule are one and the same. And now, whispers among the merchants suggest donations, favors, protections offered to those who show allegiance."

The minor lords shifted uncomfortably at this but remained silent. Duke Eldric's eyes, however, narrowed faintly—not at the priests, but at the line of conversation.

Leonid exhaled slowly, his voice quiet but firm. "You believe this to be coordinated?"

"I believe," Reginald answered carefully, "that the seeds are being planted. And others—nobles included—may be watching, waiting, weighing which path offers them greater gain."

Leonid allowed a brief pause before replying. "You speak cautiously, Chancellor."

Reginald bowed his head slightly. "I speak only out of duty, Your Majesty. I do not accuse. But I fear that if this is allowed to fester, the foundation of your reign may be tested in ways more difficult to contain than yesterday's disquiet."

Leonid's eyes briefly flicked toward Duke Eldric, gauging the man's unreadable expression, before returning to Reginald.

"And your solution?"

Reginald straightened slightly, as though bracing himself.

"We must move preemptively. The Lindin Church has established a presence in our Kingdom. Its influence runs deep, and its reach is strong. If you ask them to perform a formal inquisition—modest at first—we could root out those promoting foreign influence under the guise of faith. Quietly. Surgically. Before they gain further traction."

The word inquisition settled in the air like the first crack of distant thunder—still far off, but undeniable.

Duke Eldric finally spoke, his voice smooth and measured. "An inquisition may invite as much trouble as it seeks to quell, Chancellor. Even the smallest hint of royal persecution could embolden your enemies rather than weaken them."

"I do not suggest wide persecution," Reginald countered calmly. "Only that we employ our loyal clergy to investigate. Discreetly. With care."

Leonid remained silent for a moment, his fingertips brushing idly against the carved wood of his chair arm.

"An inquisition is a sword, Chancellor," he said softly. "Sharp? Yes. One can wield it carefully—for a time... but it cuts freely when loosened, knowing neither lord nor enemy apart."

Reginald nodded once but did not retreat. "Better to hold the hilt now, Your Majesty, before another takes it from your hand."

Leonid stood slowly. The nobles rose instinctively with him.

He moved forward, past Reginald, pausing near the window, his gaze falling on the distant spires beyond.

"Not yet," he said at last. "We are not so far lost that we must light fires to burn away our own people."

His voice was calm—but final.

Duke Eldric dipped his head in acknowledgment, his eyes unreadable.

Reginald bowed once more. "As you command, Your Majesty."

Leonid turned back toward them, his face serene.

"See that order remains in the capital. No foreign clergy will be permitted beyond their current allowance. But no inquisition will begin without my word."

Leonid began to raise his hand to release the nobles. Duke Eldric, recognizing his intent, spoke out.

"Your Majesty," he began. He smiled gently. "If you permit, I'd like to bring us to another topic."

"Speak," Leonid said simply.

Eldric moved a step closer. Close enough to feel more intimate than before, but still within respectable bounds.

"If you will, Your Majesty, I'd like to ask of your plans for your marriage," he began. He turned towards Reginald to see if he would be intercepted again.

Leonid preempted him by silently signaling to Reginald to keep his peace.

"Are you asking if I have considered your proposal to bring the wedding to a closer date?"

Eldric bowed in acknowledgement.

"I have considered. Your suggestion and arguments made sense," he began.

A smile grew on Eldric's face.

"But."

Eldric froze.

"After the events of yesterday, I am considering holding off until well after my Coming of Age ceremony."

Eldric's, mouth dropped open. He stammered. "Your Majesty, you've heard my reasoning. My argument against your having to wait. You've already been crowned. Your Coming of Age ceremony is but a formality and has no effect on your status as the sovereign of this kingdom. Why would you—"

"Because that's what I've decided," Leonid said quietly, cutting off Eldric.

Before the man could respond, Leonid began to walk off towards the large window again. He waved his hand over his shoulder.

The meeting was dismissed.

As the nobles filed out quietly, only Reginald lingered for a breath longer. His eyes met Leonid's — a silent exchange that neither voiced aloud. The Chancellor bowed deeply, and withdrew.

And Leonid stood alone for a moment longer in the silence, watching the banners sway gently outside.

Chapter 3

The council hall was alive with low murmurs as Leonid entered, flanked by his knights but walking without ceremony. The minor lords rose respectfully at his presence, though their bows carried just a fraction less humility than before.

Duke Eldric was already seated, his posture relaxed, one leg crossed over the other as though this chamber were his drawing room. His eyes met Leonid's with composed politeness.

Leonid took his place at the head of the crescent table, fingers folding lightly together upon the polished surface.

The chamberlain's voice rang out crisply. "My Lords, His Majesty invites your counsel."

For a moment, no one spoke.

Then Lord Fenric, a merchant-lord whose wealth had grown steadily in recent years, leaned forward.

"My Liege," Fenric began with the smooth confidence of one unaccustomed to refusal. "As always, we are honored to serve. Yet... concerns have been raised among the guilds."

Leonid's head tilted slightly. "Concerns?"

Fenric nodded, his smile carefully measured. "The incident during the festival—while minor, thankfully—did reveal certain... instabilities within the capital. The common folk are restless. Foreign influences spread unchecked. Some among the guilds fear that continued unrest could disrupt trade, confidence, and stability."

"And your solution?" Leonid asked evenly.

"Modest reforms," Fenric offered quickly. "Greater oversight of marketplaces. Temporary tariffs on imported goods—particularly those linked to foreign faiths. Perhaps even... restricting public processions without royal sanction."

Leonid allowed the words to sit in the air for a moment.

"Modest," he repeated softly.

"It would show strength, Your Majesty," Lord Fenric pressed, emboldened. "The people crave reassurance."

"And yet," Leonid said, "such 'modest' actions would likely provoke fresh outcries. Whispers of oppression. Discontent from those who feel targeted."

Fenric's eyes flickered for a moment, but he recovered smoothly. "If their loyalty lies within our borders, they will understand."

At the far end of the table, Duke Eldric cleared his throat gently. "Your Majesty, might I offer a thought?"

Leonid gestured permission.

Eldric rose from his seat with an easy grace. "My cousin's wisdom serves him well." The compliment was a blade hidden in silk.

Reginald stepped forward quickly. His voice burst forth. "You will address his Highness properly."

Leonid's hand raised partially from the surface of the table. Reginald, aware of the signal, stepped back.

Eldric, eyes fixed to Leonid, waited until Leonid gave a subtle nod. He bowed his head and continued as though Reginald's interruption hadn't occurred.

"But one must consider appearances carefully. The world watches. So do our neighbors." He folded his hands behind his back. "Too swift a hand might invite whispers that even your own subjects doubt your rule."

Leonid's gaze didn't waver. "You believe restraint serves us better, cousin?"

Eldric offered a faint, perfectly neutral smile. "Balance, Your Majesty. Neither weakness nor provocation."

The chamber fell still again.

From Leonid's right, Chancellor Reginald stepped forward, breaking the silence with his quiet gravity. "Your Majesty, foreign eyes indeed watch us. Yet so do foreign agents. We must not allow the liberties granted by your mercy to be twisted into instruments of sedition."

Leonid raised a hand lightly. "Enough."

The room fell silent.

He rose from his chair, voice steady, eyes sweeping each of them in turn.

"I hear your concerns. And I do not dismiss them." His tone remained calm but unmistakable. "But I will not be goaded into foolish haste. There will be no blanket restrictions. No tariffs. No decrees driven by fear."

He paused, letting the weight of his words settle.

"We govern by law, not panic."

The minor lords bowed quickly, though some stiffly. Lord Fenric's eyes lowered with a hint of frustration. Eldric, as always, maintained his unreadable smile.

Leonid's voice softened, but sharpened beneath the surface.

"If any among the noble houses believe themselves better suited to rule, let them speak plainly rather than stir unrest behind closed doors."

A hush spread across the chamber.

When none dared reply, Leonid's voice lowered another fraction. "Good. Then I trust this council remains loyal."

The nobles murmured in assent, and Leonid slowly sank back into his chair.

"Chancellor," he said softly. "See that peace holds."

"As you command, Your Majesty."

The meeting slowly dissolved as the nobles retreated from the chamber. Eldric was last to leave, offering only a final courteous bow before slipping into the shadowed corridor beyond.

Leonid remained seated for some time afterward, his fingers lightly drumming against the carved edge of the table. Eventually he retired to his study.

The study was dimmer than usual. Heavy clouds rolled across the afternoon sky, muting the light through the tall windows. Flickering candlelight cast long shadows against the pale stone walls. The scent of lavender still hung faintly in the air, mingling with the faint musk of old parchment.

Leonid stood by the window, hands clasped behind his back, his reflection caught faintly in the glass. The distant rooftops of the capital spread below him, quiet for the moment, but restless beneath the surface.

Isolde entered softly, closing the door behind her. Her gown whispered across the polished floor as she approached.

"You summoned me, my king?" she asked with quiet warmth, a playful lilt beneath the formality.

Leonid smiled faintly, but his gaze remained distant for a moment longer. "I only wished for your company."

Isolde moved closer, her hand lightly brushing along his sleeve before slipping into his grasp.

"They speak of you, you know," she whispered.

Leonid finally turned his full attention to her. "Who?"

"The merchants. The guildmasters. Even the lower nobles." She paused, searching his face carefully. "There are whispers, Leonid. Rumors spreading like ivy across the walls."

He drew a slow breath. "I hear them too. But rumors are currency in court. That currency is always spent carelessly."

Isolde's lips pressed together. "These rumors grow more organized. Some speak of Uriliation quietly in noble halls. Of how certain houses would prosper under new alliances. Of how you are... young."

Leonid's voice, when it came, remained steady. "And yet none dare say it aloud."

"Not yet," she agreed softly. "But the knife they prepare will not strike openly." She drew closer, resting her head briefly against his shoulder. "They will press the people first. Use unrest. Use fear."

Leonid's hand rose, gently stroking her hair. "I'd rather they speak to me from my face, not my back."

"I know," she whispered. "But you must be ready."

He looked down at her now — not as sovereign to subject, but as equal to equal. "You would have me strike first?"

"No." She met his gaze with unwavering certainty. "I would have you be ready. I know you won't strike preemptively."

Leonid studied her for a long moment. "It does not trouble you to speak of such things?"

"Of course it does." Her voice softened. "But I will not pretend that soft words alone will shield us."

The silence stretched between them for a breath, charged but not heavy.

Finally, Leonid spoke, his voice low.

"They call me young. Naive. They see a boy wearing his father's crown."

Isolde's fingers tightened slightly around his hand.

Leonid's eyes sharpened. "But I know who I am."

He leaned forward, voice almost a whisper — not boastful, not bitter. Simple fact.

"I am Innocence."

Isolde's breath caught slightly at the words. She understood — not innocence as they imagined it. Not childishness. But the purity of conviction, uncorrupted by the rot of cowardice or compromise.

He continued softly. "And because I am Innocence, they think me harmless. They only see weakness."

Her eyes glimmered. "Let them."

Leonid smiled faintly, and pulled her fully into his embrace.

Isolde hesitated before speaking again, lowering her voice even further as though the stone walls themselves might betray her.

"Leonid... my father gave me a request. A demand, really."

Leonid's brow lifted faintly. "Go on."

"He told me to press the issue of our marriage. To make you give in. He wants the wedding soon—as soon as possible."

For a long moment, Leonid said nothing. No flicker of irritation, no sign of anger clouded his expression. When he finally answered, his voice was calm.

"We're still children, Isolde. You thirteen, me fourteen. What sense does that make?" he paused. Taking a moment to lose himself in her eyes. "But—if that's what you want... I'll do it."

She stepped forward, closing the last distance between them. One hand rested lightly on his chest as she laid her head against him.

"I want you," she whispered. "That's all. I know what my father wants. Closer ties to the throne. Our royal blood is generations thin. His plan is likely this: 'If something happens to you, our side of the royal blood — thin as it may be — can assume the throne.'"

Leonid exhaled slowly, lowering his head against hers.

"Then we will give him nothing."

Leonid remained in his study. Isolde had left hours earlier. The study was quiet save for the faint crackle of the hearth. The tall windows stood open to the evening breeze, letting in the soft scents of lavender from the castle gardens. The amber glow of lanterns illuminated the shelves of old tomes that lined the chamber, their leather spines worn smooth with generations of use.

Leonid sat at the center table, his fingertips resting lightly against one another, eyes distant but alert. The day had been long. The council meetings taxing. But this was not a conversation that could wait.

Chancellor Reginald stood before him, hands folded behind his back. The older man's face was lined with quiet tension, though he maintained his usual tone of polite deference.

"Your Majesty," Reginald began carefully, "my agents have returned with troubling reports."

Leonid's gaze shifted. "Spies."

Reginald blinked, caught briefly off guard. "I beg your pardon, Sire?"

Leonid's voice remained soft, but firm. "Call them what they are, Chancellor. We deal in truth here."

Reginald hesitated, then dipped his head slightly. "Very well, Your Majesty. My spies report that someone within the noble class is using the growing unrest surrounding the Uriliation priests for personal advantage."

Leonid said nothing, waiting.

Reginald continued. "It is unclear who precisely moves the pieces, but their hand is becoming bolder. Money is changing hands. Meetings are being held in private estates outside the city proper. Certain merchant houses appear increasingly aligned with the priests' supporters. And the commoners whisper."

The quiet stretched.

"You must do something, my Lord," Reginald finally pressed, his voice heavier now. "If things continue as they are, this will slip beyond our reach."

Leonid exhaled slowly, eyes narrowing. "I know this."

"Do you have a plan, Sire?"

Leonid's fingers tapped once against the table. "It is not a question of having a plan. I hesitate. That is all."

Reginald stepped forward a pace, his voice tightening. "Hesitation is a luxury we may soon lose. There are options before us."

Leonid's head inclined slightly. "Go on."

Reginald drew a measured breath. "We could move a portion of the army into the city. Quietly. Their mere presence would suppress potential riots before they spark. A demonstration of strength—subtle but effective."

Leonid's brow furrowed, his voice calm but sharper now. "No."

Reginald's hands clenched briefly. "Why not? It is a simple precaution. We do not need to wield the sword—only show that we still hold it."

Leonid sat back, folding his arms across his chest, voice lowering to a steady rhythm. "The soldiers defend our borders from the enemy without. If we turn them inward, we declare that the people themselves are now the enemy. An enemy within."

He paused, letting Reginald absorb the full meaning of that statement before continuing. "Once that line is crossed, Chancellor, it does not return easily."

Reginald's jaw tightened. Reginald's jaw tightened. He rubbed his brow, paced briefly, then crossed to the side table where a small decanter waited. He poured himself a short drink, downing it quickly.

The silence pulsed between them for a moment more.

"You are not wrong, Sire," Reginald said at last, his voice quieter. "But inaction carries risk of its own. Your enemies—whoever they are—move freely while we debate virtue."

Leonid watched him evenly. "And yet virtue is all that keeps us from becoming as dangerous as those who seek to unseat us."

Reginald nodded once, though his shoulders remained tight.

"I serve at your will, Your Majesty."

Leonid stood slowly, signaling the conversation was over. "We will hold the army at the borders. Let the people see that their king still trusts them."

Reginald bowed, deeply this time. But as he turned to leave, his features betrayed the growing worry he carried. The door closed quietly behind him, leaving Leonid once again alone with the flicker of the firelight.

The quiet was complete.

And still, the pressure outside continued to rise.

"This will not be all," Leonid whispered into the silence.

Chapter 4

It was almost a week later. Just barely six days had passed. The council chamber carried a different tension this morning. Gone was the polite air of minor grievances and ceremonial updates. The air felt tighter—dense, as though the stone walls themselves leaned inward, listening.

Leonid sat at the head of the long polished table, his gaze cool as he watched the men gather. Isolde sat to his left. Reginald stood to his right, as always, his expression calm but tense. A few trusted minor lords filled the remaining seats — those who had proven loyal thus far. Duke Eldric was last to enter, moving with the same practiced dignity as always, though today there was a certain deliberate slowness to his steps. Calculated. Intentional.

"My Lords," Leonid began, his voice calm, "we proceed directly to the matter at hand."

Reginald stepped forward. "The reports have grown troubling, Your Majesty."

He placed several sealed letters on the table. "Multiple sources confirm what we feared. Several merchant guilds have split their loyalties. The Uriliation faction's financial supporters have increased their offerings."

Leonid offered no immediate response, his eyes merely shifting to the documents.

Reginald continued. "The foreign priests grow bolder. Sermons speak openly now of divine mandate. They do not name Your Majesty directly... but the implication is clear. There are whispers of 'restoring spiritual order,' of bringing the throne under proper faith."

One of the minor lords shifted uncomfortably in his seat but said nothing.

Reginald's tone tightened. "Additionally, Your Majesty... arms shipments have quietly moved through certain coastal holdings.

Nobles allied with the dissenters deny any involvement, but their household guards have grown considerably in number."

A brief pause followed. Reginald shifted his gaze across the individuals in the room. His eyes didn't stay long on any one individual, but some nobles were quick to divert their gaze under the scrutiny. The implication pressed into the chamber.

Then, softly, Duke Eldric finally spoke.

"Your Majesty... surely you see the pattern emerging."

Leonid's gaze moved to him, calm as still water.

Eldric's smile was faint, careful. "Your reign is young, your rule... still finding its strength. No man questions your bloodline. But at times like these, stability becomes fragile. Dangerous elements may test the order that holds this kingdom together."

"And what would you propose, cousin?" Leonid asked.

"A firm hand," Eldric answered. "Decisive action. Before those who plot can make their move. You must show the people that your rule is unshakable—that the crown is not subject to squabbling priests or self-serving merchants."

Leonid gave no outward reaction, letting him continue.

Eldric's voice lowered slightly, as if offering counsel more than challenge. "If necessary, a quiet... restructuring of certain alliances might bring fresh unity. Stronger ties between your house and others. Marital ties, perhaps, should not wait for formal ceremonies." His eyes flicked towards his daughter.

Leonid glanced toward Isolde from the corner of his eye. She remained still.

Leonid's fingers idly traced the carved stag on the armrest of his chair. "You return, again, to the matter of the wedding."

Eldric bowed his head faintly. "The timing is fortuitous. A completed union would quiet many doubters. It signals permanence, strength, maturity."

Leonid studied him a long moment. "I did not know you viewed your daughter's hand as a shield for my throne."

Eldric didn't flinch. "I view my daughter as a gift to this kingdom. Her loyalty to you is absolute. And my loyalty... follows."

The meaning beneath the words settle thick in the air.

Reginald's jaw stiffened slightly, but he held his tongue.

Leonid looked to his left. "What say you, my Lady?"

The chamber held its breath as Isolde's eyes dropped to her folded hands. Much too focused for a child so young. When she spoke, her voice barely rose above a whisper, but it carried like a hammer-fall in the quiet hall.

"Your will is my will, Your Majesty," she said simply.

Eldric's eye twitched — quickly buried. Leonid caught it.

His brow lifted. "There you have it, cousin."

The word cousin landed hollow. Normally a mark of kinship. Here, stripped of warmth. Blood, yes—but no station. No standing. Only distance.

His daughter did not respond as he'd hoped. Undeterred, Eldric said, "Is this your answer, Your Majesty?"

Leonid finally spoke, voice even, soft. "What you offer sounds more like positioning than loyalty."

"My loyalty is pragmatic," Eldric answered, his tone respectful but clear. "As all loyalty must be."

Silence settled once again.

Leonid broke it at last, addressing Reginald rather than Eldric. "The reports—is it your belief that we face open rebellion?"

"Not yet, Your Majesty," Reginald answered carefully. "But... we stand at its threshold."

Leonid nodded once, absorbing the words fully.

Duke Eldric allowed himself a final step closer, speaking now with calculated gravity. "Do not wait until it becomes impossible to act without bloodshed."

He pointed towards his daughter. "Do not force those who care for you, and for this realm, to choose between love and necessity."

Leonid's eyes lifted slowly to meet his cousin's gaze.

"Thank you for your counsel, cousin," he said quietly. "I will consider what you've offered."

The Duke bowed with practiced grace, but beneath it, a predator's stillness remained.

Leonid waved his hand. "You are all dismissed."

The minor lords departed quickly. Eldric was last to turn away, his steps measured, unhurried.

Only Reginald remained, waiting for his king's final word. But Leonid offered none. He merely stared past the chamber's tall windows, watching storm clouds gather at the distant horizon.

The heavy doors to the council chamber closed behind them, muffling the echo of departing footsteps. The hall beyond lay quiet, save for the flicker of torchlight against marble walls.

Leonid walked ahead in silence, hands clasped behind his back. Isolde followed, careful not to break his quiet, though her gaze never left him.

As they neared his private chambers, the attendants waiting outside stepped forward instinctively. Leonid offered no words, only a single glance. The kind that needed no repetition. The servants bowed and withdrew immediately, including Isolde's Lady-in-waiting who had followed them.

The moment the doors closed behind them, the quiet shifted. Private. Intimate.

Leonid moved to the edge of his bed and reclined, propping himself up on one elbow. His posture appeared casual, but Isolde saw through it. She stepped closer, standing beside him.

"Don't stay up late thinking too much again," she said, the corners of her lips lifting slightly, echoing their familiar teasing.

Leonid didn't answer at first. His eyes traced the ceiling beams before settling on her face.

"I'm not thinking about anything," he said softly. "Except you."

She arched a brow with faint amusement, but her hand found his. "Flatterer."

He tugged gently on her wrist, inviting her down beside him. She accepted, settling beside him atop the bed, shoulder to shoulder, their hands remaining linked.

For a long moment, neither spoke.

It was Isolde who broke the silence.

"What troubles you, Leonid? Truly."

He stared upward a moment longer before answering, voice steady.

"I told you — the decisions ahead don't trouble me. They never have."

Isolde turned her head slightly, resting her cheek against his shoulder. Her voice came quiet, but resolute.

"Whatever must be done, will be done. I know you won't act from pride. Or greed. Or fear. That's why I trust you."

He inhaled slowly. "If I act, I act, Isolde. Will it trouble you if I do?"

"No," she whispered. "It won't."

Leonid sat up. His tone shifted.

"I've found evidence your father's behind the Uriliantian priests entering the kingdom. Does that change your response?"

Isolde shook her head. "It doesn't."

Leonid nodded once. "Alright. I understand now."

He rang a small bell. Moments later, an attendant opened the doors.

"Send for the Chancellor."

Reginald arrived swiftly, bowing as he entered. Leonid stood at the center of the chamber, voice calm, but distant — as though speaking from across some unseen divide.

"I shall do as my father taught me," Leonid said softly.

Reginald stiffened at the tone. He glanced around the room instinctively, half-expecting a chill.

"This is a card I can only play once," Leonid continued. "Once done, it can never be used again."

Reginald swallowed. "What card, Your Majesty?"

Leonid turned to face him fully.

"I will not be a tyrant. But tyranny has its use. When it comes, it must strike swiftly. Absolutely. Without hesitation. As a statement none can ignore — and none will defy."

Reginald's throat worked nervously. The look in Leonid's eyes was something unfamiliar. Not rage. Not desperation.

Certainty.

Leonid stepped closer, voice steady.

"Gather the army. March on the Duke's territory."

Reginald's brow lifted slightly. "Duke Eldric?"

Leonid placed a hand on Reginald's shoulder. He nodded.

"Raze it to the ground. Leave nothing alive. Not Duke Eldric. Nor women, children. The old. The young. I don't even want a dog to survive."

Reginald's mouth parted, stunned. His gaze fixed on Leonid's eyes. What he found there was... a grief that had long since resolved itself.

Only now did Reginald understand: Leonid had not *just decided this*. He was never *deciding* anything. The choice had been made long ago. Now—he only set aside his mourning of it.

This wasn't the moment Leonid became king. He *was* king.

Reginald finally recognized who had always been seated on the throne.

The Chancellor stood frozen, helpless before the revelation. A boy. A king. Not separated by time, waiting to catch up to the weight of the crown. He waited to be revealed by issuing one command.

Leonid turned to Isolde.

"Do you hate me?"

Her gaze shifted, just slightly—toward the empty air where her father's name still lingered.

A breath. Nothing more.

She shook her head. "Your will is my will, Your Majesty."

She stood and moved beside him, embracing him softly.

"Don't fear what the masses will say," she whispered. "A man who kills another is a killer. A killer of ten is a serial killer—"

Leonid finished the thought, "And a killer of a hundred is a butcher."

Isolde placed her hand on his chest.

Her eyes met his.

Unyielding. Cavernous. Beautiful.

"Yes," she whispered. "But a killer who slays a thousand..."

She leaned into him, resting her head lightly against his chest.

"...is called a hero."

Afterword: The Boy, the Crown, and You

This was never a story about kingdoms.

Not really.

It wore the costume of political drama—chancellors, councils, processions, religious tension—but none of that was the point. Those things existed only to give context to the real thing I was asking you to see. And it wasn't power. Or war. Or destiny.

It was a boy.

A boy with a crown. A boy who never once lost control of his own narrative. A boy who invited your empathy and your trust, and who never once let go of your hand—right up to the moment he told you what he'd already decided.

That was the story.

If you found yourself connected to Leonid—if you believed in him, felt for him, wanted the best for him—good. That means I did my job. Because I built this piece with one purpose in mind: **to draw you into alignment with a character so deeply, so quietly, that by the time you realized what he was capable of, you couldn't pull away.**

And then I wanted you to ask yourself: *what now?*

What do you do with that connection?

What do you do when a character you trusted does something you might not have approved of—if you'd seen it coming?

What do you do when the emotional part of you still understands him, even as the logical part of you wants to step away?

These are the questions this story was written to ask. Not of the characters. Of **you**.

How I Pulled It Off

I'll tell you how I did it, since you're here. Since you trusted me enough to follow this far.

I began with **character before plot**. That's the entire trick. Everything else is scaffolding.

I made Leonid:

· Young enough to be underestimated.

· Quiet enough to be read as contemplative.

· Emotionally expressive enough to feel accessible—but never indulgent.

Then I gave him:

· **No arc.** He doesn't change. *You do.*

· **No hesitation.** His conflict is never about what to do. It's about what it will cost—and he already knows.

· **No defense.** He never justifies himself. He never explains. You filled in the blanks. You gave him softness, mercy, hesitation—because that's what you wanted to see.

I gave him a mirror in Isolde—poised, graceful, emotionally articulate. Her loyalty wasn't submission. It was complicity born of full awareness. She never needed to rebel. She already knew who he was. She just chose him anyway.

As for the story? The rebellion, the priests, the nobles, the politics—that was **set dressing**. Functional. Convincing. But not important.

All of that was there to build a believable world so that the real experiment could work:

What happens when you align with a character so fully that their choices become your own?

And more importantly:

What does that say about how we read character at all?

Why It Matters

This wasn't a twist-ending story. It wasn't trying to pull the rug out from under you. It was trying to *move the rug* slowly—inch by inch—until you realized you weren't standing where you thought you were.

This was about **resonance**.

About connection.

About complicity.

Because fiction isn't just entertainment. It's a mirror. And when we see ourselves in a character, we're also forced to examine *why*—especially when that character turns, and we turn with them.

So if you felt betrayed at the end—good.

If you still believed in him—good.

If you're uncomfortable about either of those things—better still.

That discomfort is not a flaw in the story.

It **is** the story.

A Gift From Heaven

Let me recount a tale from thirteen years past, a tale that may challenge belief yet remains true. The story commences on a radiant night when stars congregated in the heavens to engage in their eternal dance, a celestial ritual since time's dawn. This night, they descended from their joyous revelry to gaze upon the realm below—the realm of humankind. They smiled upon this world, casting their luminance upon it as they twirled and danced through the nocturnal expanse.

Their eyes twinkled like gems, and their smiles radiated brilliance. With every laugh that escaped their celestial lips, their luminosity intensified. Amidst their mirth, they nearly missed a lone young man who emerged, his gaze drawn upwards to the heavens.

He stared at the heavens with a poignant yearning. Each star sensed his wonderment at their jubilant dance, perceiving the depth of his yearning yet unable to grasp its nature. As his outstretched hand reached for the sky, he closed his fist as if it could ensnare one of these splendid stars. Again and again he repeated this gesture. An endless game he played with the stars.

But the stars evaded his grasp, dancing in the sky, laughter ringing as they eluded his attempts. "Why do you seek to capture us from the night's embrace?" they inquired.

With a slow lowering of his hand, his open palm revealed emptiness, his expression tinged with sadness. Once more, his gaze sought the heavens, and he cried out with a voice meant for the stars to hear. "I possess an enduring love, sons who will carry my legacy, and more, yet I remain discontent."

The stars twinkled synchronously, their collective voices a harmonious chorus. "What is your quest when you possess all this? Is it riches, gold, diamonds, the adoration of the masses, or the allure of fame?"

His retort resounded, "None of these do I seek. My beloved fills me more than wealth, her permanence rivals gold, and her radiance outshines diamonds. My sons' admiration satisfies my longing, while glory and fame, bestowed by kin, need no pursuit."

Within the sky, stars weaved intricate patterns, uncertain of the man's intent in reaching so fervently from Earth to sky. They twirled and collided, their brightness compelling the man to shield his eyes.

However, within this captivating scene, an even more extraordinary moment unfurled. The moon, cloaked in her ethereal beauty, turned her gaze upon the man, a single query escaping her lips, "If you lack for naught, then what is it you truly seek? For one cannot seek without knowing what is needed."

With head bowed in contemplation, the man pondered, night cloaking his thoughts. As stars continued their celestial waltz, he gazed upward again, ready to speak. "You are right, Moon Goddess. The need eludes me, but desire, I believe, I can discern."

A radiant smile graced the man's lips, his joy mirroring the stars' merriment. His infectious smile kindled the heavens' laughter. Extending his hands, he spoke resolutely, "In my abundance, I wish to give back. A solitary request I make of you and these celestial stars: aid me in bestowing beauty upon the world."

The Moon Goddess bestowed a tender smile, commanding him, "Open your hands."

He complied, palms extended skyward, receptive to the gift from the Moon Goddess and stars. The Moon Goddess focused her ethereal light upon the brightest star, guiding its descent into the man's open palms. Her luminance caressed the star, illuminating his hands, and she bade him farewell.

"Go forth and plant this seed with your beloved. Come morn, you shall find what you truly need," she whispered softly.

Grateful, he departed, journeying to his nearby abode. Summoning his wife, they together planted the gifted seed, a gesture infused with shared intent. With the moon as their silent witness, they retired for the night.

As dawn painted the sky, cries of a newborn reached their ears. Hurriedly, they ventured to the garden, where lay the most exquisite infant girl. As the man lifted the babe, his pride emanated like sunlight.

"What name shall grace her?" inquired the wife.

A moment of reflection yielded a smile, as sweet as the babe's own. "Let us meld our names, thus she shall be known as..."

To our beloved daughter, Jaye-Lynn.

Postscript: On Building Characters

The Lesson

Todd leaned his head into his hand. His elbow was propped up on the desk he sat behind. Around him, a soft buzz of conversation filled the lecture hall.

He glanced up at the clock mounted prominently on the front wall: 7:15. No professor yet.

The registrar's office had clearly posted the start time for every class. Adherence was expected. Start late, and you challenged the illusion of order—a fragile system built to maintain control over a chaotic world.

The voices around him ebbed and flowed, waves of idle chatter filling the space. Todd's gaze drifted towards the windows. Still resting below the horizon, waiting for its cue to begin the slow climb toward noon.

He sighed.

There wasn't even a sign there would be a professor at all.

His reverie broke with the soft squeak of door hinges. Someone was coming in.

Another student?

The professor?

Maybe even a student assistant with news the class was cancelled?

His hopes were confirmed and dashed in the same breath.

The professor ambled in. Conversation died as he made his way to the center of the blackboard. Without so much as a greeting—or even an explanation for his tardiness—he reached for a piece of chalk and studied it.

He examined it as if judging whether it was worthy to serve. After a brief inspection, he seemed satisfied. Like every other piece in the tray, it would do.

Todd watched the professor's back, irritation rising. The man had been late—without so much as an acknowledgement—and now offered no explanation at all. Not even the courtesy of a simple apology.

Without further comment, the professor turned and began sketching something on the board. Then, as if belatedly remembering his audience, he spoke over his shoulder:

"Stop me as soon as you recognize what I'm drawing."

Todd blinked. *What the hell?*

He mouthed the words silently. *I thought this was a creative writing class, not a damn art class.*

He glanced around, checking to see if anyone else shared his confusion.

Within moments, a female student behind him spoke up. The professor hadn't drawn much at all.

"It's an elephant, sir."

The professor put the chalk down immediately. He didn't even bother finishing the sketch, nor did he glance back at his unfinished work.

Todd's brow pinched as he stared at the board.

How the hell did she know it was an elephant?

He turned to look at the girl who had spoken, but as he shifted back to face the front, another thought surfaced.

Why the hell hasn't anyone addressed the other elephant in the room? Why he was late? Why he hasn't even really spoken to us? And what the hell is he doing?

Those questions remained unanswered. Unacknowledged.

The professor had moved to the lectern positioned off to the side of the raised dais. The place where the lesson should have begun.

He leaned forward. Hands resting on the edge, waiting.

Todd's gaze drifted back to the blackboard. He studied the crude outline. Now that it had been named, he could almost see it—almost. A vague blob that vaguely suggested what it was meant to be.

It wasn't very good at all. From Todd's perspective, it had looked like a balloon at first—until the professor started drawing what was presumably the trunk. Then it had devolved into something resembling puffy clouds meant to pass for a body and legs. One thing was certain: It didn't look much like a goddamn elephant.

"You call that an elephant?" Todd blurted before he even realized he'd spoken. The sarcasm in his voice barely concealed the simmering frustration beneath it.

The professor glanced back at the board, surveying his crude creation. He shook his head. "Yeah, that's a damn ugly elephant, I'll admit. But in my defense, I'm not an artist."

"So what was the purpose of doing that, then?" Todd asked.

The professor paused, as if weighing how much to reveal. He could have explained everything—but instead, after a glance at his pitiful sketch, he simply said:

"One bite at a time."

Todd's mouth dropped open. He stared at the professor in bafflement until it became overwhelmingly clear that no further explanation was coming. His eyes swept across the classroom, scanning his fellow students to see if anyone else understood what was happening.

As if on cue—adding one final layer of absurdity—the professor spoke again.

"I'm not going to hold you up for the entire class today. I'm only making one point. If you've understood the lesson, you're free to leave at any time."

It didn't take long.

The female student who had first recognized the elephant stood up and quietly began packing her things. She offered no comment, no questions—just a simple nod to the teacher as she left the room.

One by one, others followed her lead.

Soon, Todd found himself alone, the professor still watching him with a curious expression. After a few moments, even the professor turned away, glanced once more at the crude drawing on the board, and muttered loud enough for Todd to hear.

"That's one damn ugly elephant."

He calmly exited afterwards, leaving Todd sitting in the empty room.

Todd shook his head, muttering under his breath, "What the hell is this? Wasn't this supposed to be a creative writing class?"

Author's Comments:

You may ask yourself, *"What was that? Was it a narrative parable? Was it a meta-lesson about writing itself?"* — and you'd be right to do so.

First, let's review some limits and boundaries.

<u>What I'm not trying to do:</u>

- I'm not trying to teach you how to write, develop a plot, cover beginnings, middles, and endings.

- I'm not trying to teach you structure, grammar, or dialogue.

- I'm not telling you that you have to build characters and treat characters the way I do.

<u>What I am trying to do:</u>

- Remind you that writers don't start with clear pictures of their settings, characters, world, world logic, plots, subplots... the list goes on.

- Tell you that we do start with vague blobs—ugly elephants.

- Share that we have to live with those incomplete pictures and keep drawing, layering, refining, and chipping away until we see the image beneath the madness.

Now, let me explain what this story was, and why it fits beautifully:

The story relates to writing in just about every way you can imagine. For instance, you begin that 100k rough draft one step at a time. You start that chapter, that scene, that line — one word at a time. None of it appears magically on the page. Writing doesn't work like that. Don't focus on "where do I begin?"

You just — begin.

The story's core message (as it relates to character creation):

You don't create realistic characters all at once. You build them one stroke at a time — one bite at a time. That's exactly how good characterization works. You don't drop a fully-formed person onto the page. You layer small strokes:

- a nervous glance
- a half-smile that betrays insecurity
- a pause before answering
- a choice they regret
- a contradiction between what they say and what they feel

Eventually, those small, seemingly simple marks start to feel real to the reader.

The key metaphor from the story:

The professor's ugly elephant = your first draft of a character (narrative). The early reader might not see the full picture yet. But as you keep layering — revision after revision — the "elephant" emerges.

The student who recognized the elephant early: some readers instinctively connect even before the picture's fully drawn, because of small emotional cues. This is what makes strong early characterization powerful.

Also by J. A. Springs

Chronicles of Cosmic Realms
Shadows of the Forgotten Void

elctrcsheepdrmwrks (Electric Sheep Dreamworks)
Blurred Vision
Fractured
Zero One

Essays in Systems and Being
Essays in Systems and Being

The Absurdities Anthology
How Not to Find Your Local Weed-Man

The Gifted
The Untamed Force
Next Exit

The Shepherd Series
The Bad Shepherd
The Good Wolf

Standalone
Sundrops
Behind the Red Door
Boundless Fragments: A Collection of Novellas and Short Stories
Fragments of Forever

Watch for more at https://writingfortheworldpress.com.

About the Publisher

LLC. Lancaster, PA

www.writingfortheworldpress.com

Read more at https://www.writingfortheworldpress.com.